American Diaries

Celou Sudden Shout

WIND RIVER, 1826

———❦———

by Kathleen Duey

———❦———

Aladdin Paperbacks

For Richard
For Ever

First Aladdin Paperbacks edition March 1998
Copyright © 1998 by Kathleen Duey

Aladdin Paperbacks
An imprint of Simon & Schuster
Children's Publishing Division
1230 Avenue of the Americas
New York, NY 10020

The text of this book was set in Fairfield Medium
Printed and bound in the United States of America
10 9 8 7 6 5 4 3

Library of Congress Cataloging-in-Publication Data
Duey, Kathleen
Celou Sudden Shout, Wind River, 1826 / Kathleen Duey. — 1st
Aladdin Paperbacks ed.
p.   cm. — (American diaries)
Summary: In 1827 in Idaho twelve-year-old Celou Sudden
Shout, who is half French and half Shoshone, attempts to
rescue her mother and two younger brothers from the Crow
warriors who kidnapped them.
ISBN 0-689-81622-7 (pbk)
1. Shoshoni Indians—Juvenile fiction. 2. Crow Indians—
Juvenile fiction. [1. Shoshoni Indians—Fiction. 2. Crow
Indians—Fiction. 3. Courage—Fiction. 4 Kidnapping—
Fiction. 5. Indians of North America—Fiction.] I. Title.
II. Series.
PZ7.D8694Ce   1998
[Fic]—dc21   97-52936
CIP   AC

The moon is nearly full. Bī'a is tense, watching off to the southeast whenever her eyes wander from her work, looking for Papa. He should be home in a few days, if he rides straight from the rendezvous, or another week or two if he travels slowly or has trouble—or if he decides to go to one of the trading posts coming back north. There is no way to know. But he should be home soon.

We spent yesterday salvaging beaver pelts from a Crow trapper who rode through. Bī'a traded him an ax and some red beads and a little of Papa's medicinal whiskey for fifteen pelts. The man had left flesh on the skins and packed them wet—they had begun to stink. Scraping them clean was terrible work, but they are all restretched now, smoked and drying.

Bī'a and I took Mu'mbič down to the stream afterward and we washed in the cold water for an hour to get rid of the smell. Jean-Paul came later, but he would not bathe when Mother told him to. We hung Mu'mbič's cradleboard over the creek and he laughed his baby laugh, watching the leaf boats Jean-Paul sent floating past.

Jean-Paul was like his old self for a while, kind and silly, answering to the name Papa gave him. With his friends he is Ka'nu-kwac—grouse tail—for the feathers he braids into his hair now. Bī'a secretly loves this. She hates the tibo's names we have. She calls me Celou instead of Tomā', but only because I was the first and it had not yet occurred to her to fight for the names with Papa. For her sons, she wants no tibo names.

Papa nicknamed me Sudden Shout because I used to cry out when I bumped my head or fell, playing. He calls me that in jest sometimes. Bī'a hates it—a second tibo name! Tomā' was her choice for me. Cloudy. I was born on a cloudy day. Or she calls me Ba'di—daughter.

Before he left this time, Papa talked again about taking Jean-Paul to St. Louis, the big village where there are many tibos—white men and women, too, he says. He wants Jean-Paul to be educated there. Jean-Paul's writing book is nearly empty this year. I know he hides it from his friends. He does not want to go to St. Louis. I do.

I have never seen a white woman, but Papa makes them sound strange. He has told stories of how they wear sleeves that puff out like little skirts, belling down to their elbows. They wear long dresses that sometimes drag the ground. He says they walk with tiny steps and lift their skirts to keep them off the dirt. He explained corsets and I cannot believe anyone would wear such a thing. Bī'a is sure he is joking. I do not think so. I want to see St. Louis. It is in the east, where the sun rises.

Ya'mpatsi threw stones at me again two days past, when I was in the big camp waiting for Bī'a. I wish sometimes that we had an Indian father. Tsi'dzi and Na'soai are my age and should be my friends, but they are not. I asked Bī'a last night about this. She says some of the women disapprove of her marriage, others envy her blue dress and her hairpins and how Papa sometimes lets her say what she thinks even when he disagrees. I am just lonely sometimes. Bī'a says the people will get used to my blue eyes, but they won't. Jean-Paul's and Mu'mbič's are dark. They are fortunate.

Before he left for the rendezvous Papa was scolding Jean-Paul about spending so much time with his cousins and the other boys. Bī'a hates this. She never scolds us, especially Jean-Paul. She says it will break his spirit and make him a weaker warrior. But Papa wants him to be a gentleman, he says, and me to be a lady.

Mu'mbič, he says, and any more children Bī'a has, will be hers—proper Shoshone. A fair bargain, he thinks, but I see Bī'a's eyes harden when he says it. Bī'a says there are old tales of women murdering their husbands for stealing their children. Papa laughs when she warns him and jokes with her until she smiles.

Bī'a is strong. She carries as much wood as any woman I have ever seen and can lift the travois over stones when she has to. She says she will not let us go. I do not know what will happen. I want to go, but I would come back. Bī'a says some of the children do not come back. Ever. That they become white and live among the white for the rest of their lives.

As I write this, Bī'a is carrying the day's water up from the creek. I too, should be working. Jean-Paul is grazing the horses in a meadow above the tipi. He will guard them all day—or at least, he is supposed to—unless some of his friends from the big camp find him and tempt him away. Bī'a says all boys become men and do as they please. Jean-Paul has ten grasses. I have two more than that, but no one lets me do as I want.

I hear Mu'mbič murmuring in his sleep. Our dear little owl. Bī'a calls him that because she says he coos like an owl at night. Papa calls him Robert less and less often. Maybe he does mean to let Bī'a make him a Shoshone.

Bī'a's aunt told her that the buffalo hunters came home with a story to tell. They saw Blackfoot warriors two sleeps west of here. We have had no trouble with them for a long time. I hope they will not come here, especially while Papa is gone. The Blackfoot people hate us and we hate them. I do not know why. All I know is I am scared.

CHAPTER ONE

Celou leaned forward to dip the quill Papa had cut for her into the little ink bottle. The grass mat and the pine boughs beneath her buffalo robe rustled, and she could smell the sharp scent the boughs gave off. The long, wooly buffalo fur tickled at her legs as she moved.

It was going to be hot in a few hours. She had been sleeping on her robe, not under it, lately. Even up this high, the summer nights were mild. Celou liked the mountains. She liked to walk along the icy creeks, and she loved the rich piñon nuts they gathered in the fall on the rocky slopes just north of where they were now. It would not be long before it would be time to mend the nut baskets and make the trek to harvest them. Last year's nuts tasted sharp now; they were going rancid.

Celou liked this camp. They were high enough to have cool nights but low enough to be able to ride down to the Ko'gohue where it ran swift and cold over rocks that tossed the water into white froth. Wind River, the white men called it. A beautiful name. The big camp was closer to the river.

Papa had wanted them to go live with Bī'a's family while he was gone, but she had resisted it. Having a white husband made her the object of curiosity and sometimes disapproval. Women often dogged her steps through camp, tugging at her blue broadcloth hem, asking her for favors with the traders, or asking her to get them things their husbands could not.

Celou stretched. She was wearing only her deerskin dress. It was more comfortable on these hot days not to wear leggings or even moccasins. Papa would not approve, she knew. When he came back, she would have to wear what he thought proper. But for now, she was free of his stern opinions.

Bī'a had been working in the hot sun bare breasted, wearing only the split apron around her waist that most women wore in summer. Papa wanted her always to wear the broadcloth dress he had bought her, and she often did—over her soft, familiar buckskin shift, decorated with elk's teeth. That way, she could please Papa and easily slip off the stiff dress the moment he rode away to hunt or to ride the trapline.

Celou heard her mother humming outside as she worked. She was beginning to really miss Papa, Celou could tell. Bī'a had argued that they should all go to this year's rendezvous, but Papa had refused. He said the rendezvous might eventually be a place to take women and children, but it wasn't yet. There was too much drinking. The men played rough sports and gambled—and sometimes got in fights.

The whole year's take of beaver and buffalo and otter and even skunk and fox skins would be lying on the ground near Bear Lake right now, Celou knew. Her father had told her all about it. Ledgers would be out and traders would be totting up pelts brought in—and money owed for goods traded out. Goods and pelts quickly changed hands at the rendezvous.

William Ashley was a fair trader, Papa said, a good man to host the first meeting, held last summer. Most of the trappers had come. Jim Bridger would be at this year's rendezvous, and Joe Meek—many of her father's old friends. It was a little closer this year, Papa said. Last year, he had had to go a day's travel farther south to Weber River.

Celou rolled the quill between her fingers. She hoped that one summer Papa would take them all. He would take Jean-Paul, of that much she was sure. Maybe not next year, but the one after, almost certainly. Celou had wanted to go this year in particular. She wanted to see the Great Salt Lake. It was only a day or two's ride south of Bear Lake. Not a long journey at all. The salt was strong enough to sting your eyes, Papa had said; the water too bitter to drink, like the ocean. Papa had seen the ocean. He had seen everything. Celou sighed. Next year the rendezvous would probably be someplace else, far from the strange salty lake.

A flicker in the sunlight made Celou look up from her daydreaming. Her mother was ducking through the tipi door, her ragged, short hair framing her face. She straightened and looked at Celou without speaking. Then she went about her work. Bï'a almost never scolded her or her brothers for idleness or anything else, but Celou could feel her thoughts. The sun was up now. She was working hard already. There was much to be done.

Celou stood up, letting her deerskin dress fall straight before she lifted her long hair and pushed it back over her shoulders. Her father didn't like her to put grease in her hair, but when she didn't, it flew about like straw in the wind and got into her eyes when she was working. She caught it in her hands and looped it into a knot at the back of her head. There. It would slide free before long, but at least it was out of her face for now.

Celou watched as her mother leaned close to sniff at Mu'mbič in his cradleboard. She wrinkled her nose and rolled her eyes in mock disgust. Celou knew it was time to bathe her brother. But since he was sleeping peacefully through his own mess, her mother stood back again, smiling. She raised one hand and the silver bracelets Papa had given her made a musical sound Celou loved. Papa had won the bracelets from a man who had traded and traveled far to the south, across the great deserts.

"That one is dirty." Bī'a pointed at the cradleboard. "Ssst! He smells terrible."

Celou watched her mother's face, waiting for her laughter to burst through her pretense at displeasure. "He is going to grow up to be like your father," Bī'a whispered, pointing at Mu'mbič. "Afraid to bathe." She shuddered, feigning great terror.

"Papa is not *afraid*," Celou teased back. "He just does not like cold water."

Her mother raked her too-short hair back from her forehead. "He is afraid of winter baths," she said.

"He hates the cold," Celou agreed. Papa was always the first among the men and boys to swim when they traveled to hunt buffalo or elk, Jean-Paul said, but only in summer. In winter he preferred warmth to cleanliness. Celou's mother bathed more often—and made her bathe, too.

"I hope Jean-Paul will stay nearby with the horses," Celou's mother said quietly. Celou knew what she meant. Jean-Paul and his friends ran around like a pack of wolves, close on each other's heels, silent and secret in their doings. They often feigned war and fought with each other or imagined enemies. Jean-Paul was becoming serious and stern as he grew up. Celou missed the laughing little brother she had always loved.

"Soon, when you waken," Celou heard her mother crooning to Mu'mbič, making up a simple poem-song, "I will make you clean again." Her song went on, nonsense and rhythm, nothing like the intricate, many-meaning hupia the people sang about Coyote or his brother Wolf. Bī'a loved making up silly songs, and this one was particularly funny. Celou laughed, but Mu'mbič only sighed in his sleep.

"I will wash your stink away," Bī'a sang. "Then you will be fit to smell again. Fit to smell again. Mu'mbič, my son."

"Papa almost never calls him Robert anymore," Celou said, knowing her mother would smile. They both disliked the white man's name Papa had given Mu'mbič.

"Robert," her mother repeated, forcing the

unfamiliar sound from between her lips. "*Robert!* It sounds like a dog belching. At least Jean-Paul is a name one can enjoy speaking. Celou is all right, too. I don't have to burp them out like this one's. Robert. Robert!" She made her voice like a croaking frog, like someone burping after eating.

Celou hid a smile. When her mother started her silly, rude jokes, even Papa could not make her stop. "Listen to it. It is worse than that. It is like the sound of a horse that has eaten cottonwood bark to keep from starving."

Celou knew that sound—and it wasn't belching. She giggled. Her mother shook her head and her hair fanned out from her face. It was still strange for Celou to see her mother with short hair, cut unevenly with her knife on the night her uncle had been killed by the bear. Celou's father had tried to keep her from cutting her legs, too, in her grief, but she had done it while he slept. Celou had seen the scars last time they had bathed at the river. They were losing their angry pink color, fading with Bī'a's sharpest grief.

Celou corked her ink bottle and set it down. She twirled the quill in her fingers. Her mother was bending over an unfolded parfleche, quick fingers sorting through the contents without spilling them onto the deer-hide floor of the tipi. The double apron she wore swung as she moved, the soft deer hide coated with dust, her brown skin stained with blood and grease from her morning's work cutting meat.

After a few seconds, she straightened, an obsidian awl in one hand. The jet black stone shone in the oval of sunlight that poured in through the open door flap. "I have broken the metal one," she said sadly as Celou met her eyes. "I pressed too hard and the tip went through the leather and broke against the rock. It was foolish."

Celou nodded, a custom of her father's that her mother had learned, too. "Are you working on a shirt for him?"

Bī'a smiled. "Mu'mbič will need his first clothes soon."

She glanced at the quill pen, still held loosely in Celou's hand. Her eyes leaped from it to the journal, then to her daughter's face. She made a little sound of disapproval. Writing made her uneasy. It was white man's medicine.

"I am almost finished," Celou said quickly. "I only wanted to write a little. Papa said to practice."

Celou saw her mother's face soften. "There is work."

Celou nodded again. "There is always work."

Her mother turned and ducked back out the

oval opening into the sunshine. Celou put her pen away, carefully pushing the quill's delicate tip into the wad of soft buffalo fur she used to protect it, hiding it in the little cache hole she had dug beneath the edge of her pallet. She didn't think her mother would destroy the quill, but she might, if she thought the writing was making any of the spirit people angry or causing a water-ghost-woman to come around the family at night, trying to steal Celou or her brothers away.

Celou glanced upward, to the array of beaver traps and hatchets hanging from the tipi poles, high enough to keep them out of the way. Her father's traps looked solid, real, the steel oiled to keep it from rusting. Celou missed him when he was gone. She felt safer when he was at home.

A thin wailing sound startled Celou. Mu'mbič was awake! She turned to face the cradleboard. At that instant, she heard her mother's voice from outside the tipi.

"Ba'di? Celou?"

"Yes, Bī'a."

"Daughter, quiet your brother. Do not bring him out here. Hide. I see four Crow coming toward our lodge. One is the trapper from yesterday. I recognize his mare. They have painted their faces red."

CHAPTER TWO

Celou swooped across the tipi and gathered Mu'mbič into her arms as her mother ducked inside and pulled on her buckskin dress—then, quickly, her blue broadcloth. She went back out, fighting her skirt to step through the tipi door.

Celou blew lightly into Mu'mbič's ear, surprising him into silence. She looked into his dark eyes, obsidian black like their mother's. "You must be quiet," she told him, trying to sound as calm as Bī'a had. Her brother blinked and yawned, stretching inside the soft deerskin that enclosed his little body. Her mother was right. He was almost too big for the cradleboard. It would not be long before he was allowed to crawl at will around the tipi, grabbing at everything he could reach. He still nursed several times a day, but he was also eating bits of food from Bī'a's fingers.

Mu'mbič wriggled and puckered his face again,

but Celou was too quick for him. Before he could make a sound, she reached out for a bit of meat left from supper the night before and pushed a tiny piece between his lips. He tongued it, intrigued. Bī'a gave him camas root, sometimes. She had often let him suck on berries held between her fingers. Meat was a novelty to him, still.

Mu'mbič stared into Celou's eyes, and she wrinkled her nose at him. He did smell dirty. Maybe the Crow would go away quickly, and her mother could throw away the soiled moss in Mu'mbič's cradleboard and wash him and. . . .

The strangers' voices scattered Celou's thoughts. They were close to the tipi now. A horse came close, the clip-clop of its hooves hollow, menacing. Celou held her breath, willing the men to go away soon. Perhaps they just wanted to be told how to reach the big camp. Maybe they had some business with the tribe.

"A woman is trying to do her work," Celou heard her mother say in quiet, respectful Shoshone. "She must smoke this meat for her husband."

Celou listened, hearing the tension in her mother's voice. By not addressing the Crow directly, by keeping her eyes averted, she was giving them a chance to leave politely. But they did not. Celou could hear the creaking of a leather parfleche, the impatient shifting of hooves.

One of the men asked something in harsh Crow. Celou heard her mother explain that she could not understand him. Then the voices stopped. Celou let Mu'mbič chew on the side of her thumb as she carried him, crossing to stand to one side of the door.

From this angle, she could see them. They were fairly young, their faces painted red as if for war. Celou felt her knees weaken, and she held Mu'mbič closer. War paint. Why? There was no fighting now. Would they be foolish enough to start a fight so close to the big camp? Didn't they know her mother's brothers and cousins would hunt them down if they made trouble?

Celou leaned forward to see her mother. She stood not far from the opening in front of the smoke rack, using two sticks to turn the strips of meat over. Her blue dress dragged in the dirt, the already soiled hemline coated with dust.

Celou looked at the meat. Jean-Paul had killed five rabbits the day before and had come home proud and haughty. Their mother had nodded curtly, as though she had expected the gift. Jean-Paul had straightened, increasing his height by standing upon his pride.

Mu'mbič bit Celou's thumb, hard, then turned

his head to one side, spitting it out. Celou tried to make him look in her eyes again, but his face was turning rose brown and she could feel him trying to move his legs. She glanced around the tipi. He was going to be screaming in a few seconds unless she got him out and cleaned him up. Bī'a had said to hide. An infant screaming was the last thing she needed to worry about just now. And it would only reinforce the fact that they were here alone, a mother, her daughter, and her crying baby.

Celou spun around, laying the cradleboard on her buffalo robe. The woven top caught on the skin and she shoved it forward, startling Mu'mbič into another short silence. By the time his eyes had narrowed and his cheeks were beginning to flush again, she was bent over him, her fingers flying over the laces. She loosened the thongs, blowing gently first at his ear, then his chin, then his pudgy throat. "O'nha," Celou whispered, insulting him by calling him a baby. "O'nha? Or have you become de:'për? Are you going to be a boy-child? Are you brave?"

Mu'mbič closed his mouth, staring at her with wide eyes. He knew his crying was not wanted by his family. Ever since his second or third moon, he had been silenced when his crying became too loud. Celou and Jean-Paul had often drowned out his wailing with shouting and singing of their own, stopping only when he did. He had learned quickly, as all babies had to. Silence could mean life. It often did.

Celou shuddered at her own thoughts and stole a glance out the door. Her mother was still standing beside the meat racks, but now she was bent over, nudging unburned sections of wood back toward the center of the fire. As she straightened, Celou saw her hands rise and fall, twisting in grace-less, jerking gestures. They were signing. Celou reached for the twined moss basket and gathered an armload to spread on her bed. Then she looked out the door again. The Crow had his right hand raised, palm outward. He tipped one way, back the other swift as a fish darting for rocks. Celou understood the sign. He was about to ask a question.

Mu'mbič wriggled and Celou glanced down at her brother. When she looked up, her mother was answering—her hand was extended palm down, her wrist turned so that her fingers pointed to the left. She rolled her hand over, then back. The answer was no.

Celou slid Mu'mbič out of his cradleboard and onto the layer of clean moss. Gathering a handful, she wiped at his bottom, then threw the soiled moss into the little pit for refuse her mother had dug near the cookfire in the center of the tipi. Filling her mouth with water from the water basket, she warmed it, then leaned over her squirming brother again. Her ears, her whole being, was focused on the sounds a few feet outside the tipi door.

There was a rough flurry of the Crow tongue, so abrupt that it made Celou flinch when it began. She understood a few words, but no more. He was asking something, over and over. She looked out. The Crow had his right hand raised close to his shoulder, one finger extended upward. Celou shivered. He was asking about her father.

Celou squirted water between her front teeth onto her brother's belly and bottom, turning him over to wipe him dry with quick, sure strokes. She used two or three more handfuls of the spongy moss to make sure he was clean. Then she glanced out the door again.

Celou swallowed nervously. One of the Crow had gotten off his horse. He was standing close to her mother. Too close. His face was hard and emotionless. His eyes were like knife obsidian, dark and shining and cold. The fringe that hung from his white buckskin sleeves swung with every movement he made. The tips of the fringe had been painted red as though he had dipped them in blood.

Her breath as quick and light as a cornered rabbit's, Celou spilled all of the damp moss from her brother's cradleboard and repacked it with dry. He protested only a little as she placed him inside again and pulled the laces tight. Afraid to set him down, she slung the cradleboard onto her back and pulled the carry straps across her own chest.

Where is your man? the Crow was signing.

Not far, Celou saw her mother sign back. *Just over there.*

She pointed in the direction of the big camp. One of the Crow laughed, a brittle, short sound. He said something in his own language, then made a gesture that Celou knew all too well. *Blackfoot.*

Celou stared. What did he mean? There had been no danger from Blackfoot warriors for most of the summer. The hunters had seen them, but that meant nothing. They had been peaceful for a long time. That was why her father had decided they would be safe out here by themselves while he was gone. Celou stared out at the Crow warriors.

Where are your horses? the first man signed. The fringe on his shirt danced with his gestures. It was long twists of snow-white ermine skin, rolled into cords. His horse was a tall bay, big and long-legged enough to be a buffalo horse. His companions stood back, letting him deal with her mother. He was a little older than the others, perhaps.

Celou thought she understood what was going

on. The Crow had decided to steal their horses, but they hadn't been able to spot Jean-Paul up in the high meadow. But that didn't explain the warrior signing *Blackfoot*. Involuntarily, Celou's eyes sought the distant ridge that sheltered the big camp. She could not see it through the trees on the lower end of their clearing.

"My husband and brother are with the horses," Celou heard her mother lie. "And my cousins." She made signs to match her words.

There was another answering rush of Crow from the man with the reddened fringe. He half turned, and Celou saw his long hair was bound up in a bundle on the back of his neck.

One of the other men started talking; Red-fringe answered him. They were disagreeing about something. One of the others was the one who had brought the pelts, and he was turning on his horse, looking around their camp. Celou tried to recall exactly what had been said the day before when he had arrived, bearing the stinking, badly scraped beaver skins. Bī'a had shooed her and Jean-Paul inside the tipi. They had played with Mu'mbič until the Crow had left. It had been only a few minutes.

Where are your children? the Crow signed.

Celou felt her heart miss one beat, then begin again.

Where? He made the sign for a question again, his upraised hand jerking outward. He pointed in one direction, then another. The impatience in the gesture was obvious.

"I sent them to the big camp. Just over that rise," Celou's mother said. "To my mother. Their gā́ku." She pointed, repeating it in signs. Then she opened her mouth as if to say more, but the Crow warrior raised a hand to silence her, his red-tipped fringe jouncing with the movement. He reached out to take her by the arm.

Celou saw her mother pull in a deep breath. Then, without glancing back even once at the tipi, she wrenched free and began to run. She ran fast. All her life, Celou knew, her mother had won the running races—even the ones during buffalo hunt when dozens of families traveled together. She ran like the rain fell, swift and straight, her blue dress hitched up above her knees.

The Crow warriors stood still, startled, their eyes wide, as if they could not believe how swiftly she had left them, or how fast she was now making her way through the tall grass, downhill toward the band of thick pines above the creek. Then, the three who had remained on their horses whirled their mounts around and galloped off to chase her.

Celou saw her mother glance back at the

sound of hoofbeats, her hair whipping across her face. Then she veered toward the heavy timber at the lower edge of the clearing. Celou knew what her mother was thinking. If she could reach the tangled maze of logs and trees, she had a chance of outrunning the horses.

CHAPTER THREE

For the first three heartbeats, Celou was as aston-ished as the Crow warriors had been. She stood rooted to the earthen floor of the tipi, standing well back from the bright oval of the door, watching her mother fly like a deer down the hillside. Red-fringe was on his horse now, shouting at the others.

Celou's mind began to work again. Her mother had given her the only chance there was to give. She had to take it. She held still, praying to her father's God that the last Crow would join the chase. Finally, spitting into the little fire, kicking at the smoke rack to turn it over, he lashed at the tall bay's flanks, sending it into a gallop.

Freed to move at last, Celou spun around, snatching her mother's meat knife from its thong. Conscious of the weight of her brother on her back, she knelt upon her pallet and slit the deerskin liner, a curtain that was tied to the inside of the tipi poles.

Lying on her belly, one hand curved upward to make sure the cradleboard tilted down to fit, she slithered under the tipi cover.

Out in the early morning sunshine, Celou rolled to one side, then turned to reach back inside the tipi. She pulled her buffalo robe into a messy pile that would hide the slit from a casual search. Then she got to her feet and ran uphill, in the opposite direction from the one her mother had taken. She ran without glancing back, the knife still clenched in her right hand.

Celou did not stop until she had reached the first line of trees at the far edge of their meadow. She darted into the trunks and found a place to hide among the shadows, then she reached back to touch Mu'mbič's cheek with one hand. The trees made it hard, but she leaned to one side, straining to see what had happened to her mother. It was impossible. The land fell away too steeply on the far side of the tipi. She closed her eyes, trying to hear. Mu'mbič was still, probably scared from the jarring run.

At first there was only the sound of horses' hooves and a rill of dust rising like morning-fire smoke. Then there were muted shouts. Afraid to move, afraid to stay, Celou stood trembling. Small sounds drifted back to her. Her mother's cry. A laugh. A whinny cut short by the crack of a riding whip. Then silence.

Celou tried to think. This had gone beyond horse theft. She wasn't sure why, but it had. Maybe Shoshone somewhere had attacked Crow, and this was their chance to get even. Her mother was a skilled tanner of hides and a maker of good buckskin robes and shirts. Her own clothing would tell the Crow warriors this much. She was not old, and she was strong. They would probably kidnap her, not kill her.

Celou looked uphill. Jean-Paul was not too far away, straight upslope. The big camp was much farther. She might be able to reach Jean-Paul, and once they had horses, they might make it to her mother's people. Celou knew it was their best chance. She could not fight four Crow warriors. Nor could Jean-Paul. But her mother's brothers and uncles and cousins could. Or maybe, Celou let herself hope, her mother had gotten away and was even now running down the creek path toward the big camp.

Celou started uphill, then heard a shout and froze, turning back. Below her, across the clearing, she saw one of the Crow's head and shoulders rise above the crest of the hill. It was eerie, not being able to see his horse at first, as though he was some kind of spirit man, gliding over the ground. A moment later, as he came uphill, his horse's head emerged, then its chest and flanks. He cantered sideways along the slope, looking down at the ground.

Celou's reason finally pushed her fear aside. The shout had had nothing to do with her. He hadn't seen her. They were looking for tracks, now, trying to find the horses. Celou exhaled.

Her family had lived in the meadow nearly two moons, close to her mother's family for the long, hot season of Tatsa. As long as they had lived here, they had gone back and forth to the big camp, and her mother's people had come to visit every few days. Jean-Paul's friends had ridden into the meadow dozens of times. There would be many tracks, old and new, coming and going. The Crow would not likely see her bare footprints among the tufts of grass that grew from the hard, rocky ground—that wasn't what they were looking for. And they would be in a hurry if her mother had gotten away, knowing she would run for help.

Celou watched a little longer, until three of the Crow were riding back and forth across the meadow. She could not see the fourth, but he was probably just lower down, where the hill hid him. She couldn't tell from their manner if her mother had eluded them or not.

Celou stepped away from the tree she had hidden behind. She was foolish to be standing, watching. She would have a chance to warn Jean-Paul, to ride with him for help, but only if she could climb the mountainside faster than she ever had before. It would take the Crow a little time to decide which way Jean-Paul had driven the five horses early this morning, but they would puzzle it out.

Celou realized she was still grasping the knife in her right hand, and she slid it beneath her belt. Darting from one tree to the next, looking back every few seconds, she made her way uphill through the next ragged line of pines. Then, when she was sure she was well out of sight of the Crow warriors crisscrossing the meadow, she started a curve that would take her upslope.

Mu'mbič rode silently in his cradleboard. Celou could hear his small breaths, as quick and light as her own. She knew he was scared, that he felt her fear and respected it. That was good. She was proud of her brother.

The ground was rocky, and Celou quickly wished she had thought to bring her moccasins. She ran where she could, walking fast through the thick sagebrush when she could not. She kept herself going, refusing to look back until she reached a little outcropping that she knew overlooked the meadow. Only then did she risk stopping long enough to look back down at the tipi.

For an instant, her hope rose like dawn birds, then it fell again. Her mother was not running for help. She had not escaped. One of the Crow had forced her to ride behind him. Celou counted. She could still see only three of them. Where was the fourth? Already on his way up the mountainside? She scanned her side of the clearing, listening for hoofbeats and crackling brush. There was no sound.

Using her fear to drive her legs faster, Celou turned uphill and concentrated upon running. Once or twice she thought she heard distant shouts, but she did not slow. In some places, she jumped from rock to rock, staying clear of the fallen trees and brush that made running almost impossible. But mostly, she was following narrow game trails through the thick stands of sage—trying her best to keep up a good pace through the tangle of brush.

Above her, the trees thinned in places, baring the rocky earth over wide sections of the ground. Celou tried to decide. If she stayed in the thickets, she would be harder to see, but greatly slowed. When her breath began to burn, she stopped to rest and risked another look back down the mountainside.

The tipi looked small from where she now stood, dragging in one painful breath after another. The scattered stands of pine trees hid some of the meadow below. Still, she could see all four warriors now, circling at an easy lope, their spirals widening. Wherever the fourth one had been, he hadn't started upslope yet. Celou pushed her sweat-damp hair back from her face. So. She still had a chance.

Celou watched her mother riding behind the warrior with the long-fringed shirt. Her head was averted, her arms straight down at her sides. She was refusing to touch Red-fringe. The warriors rode in ever-widening circles and Celou knew they were getting closer to the game trail her brother usually headed up in the mornings. They would see the long thread of the horses' fresh tracks soon and begin to follow it.

Celou reached back over her shoulder to touch Mu'mbič's cheek again. He turned toward her thumb and she felt his warm little mouth close around it. He was hungry, but he made no sound. Singing softly to him of their mother's bravery, the words broken by her labored breathing, Celou started uphill again.

As she went, the pines thickened, then grew thin again. She took the path through the open ground, forcing herself to keep up a fast pace. Here and there a stand of aspen trees glittered in the early light, their leaves flashing as the breeze touched them.

Where the ground opened out, Celou forced herself to run, refusing to feel the bruised places on her feet and legs where she had misjudged a step.

Mu'mbič was calming. She could hear little sounds from him now. His fear was easing and she was glad for him. Her own was tightening in her stomach like a coiled snake. Every stride mattered, every step carried her closer to knowing whether or not her gamble would prove foolish. Her whole family depended upon her now.

Bursting out of the tree line into the high meadow, Celou saw the horses grazing a little distance away. She let out a little cry of relief. Mu'mbič echoed her softly, sounding once more like his namesake on a summer night.

"Little Owl," Celou said. "Little Owl, we are going to ride for help!"

She began to run again, this time with a lightness in her heart that helped lift her feet, helped the mountain air rush in and out of her lungs. Then, as she got closer, she dropped back to a walk, afraid she might spook the horses.

The roan gelding lifted his head as they came near. He had been her father's favorite horse for several years. He was big, swift, and steady. He was here only because he had had a bruised pastern a month ago, when her father had left. The small-boned mare that Celou usually rode lifted her pretty bay face above the grass. The two grays and her mother's black did not stop grazing. She could not see her brother's buckskin mare anywhere.

"Jean-Paul?" Celou called softly.

There was no answer.

Celou came forward, suddenly nearly overcome with anger. Her brother's foolishness was going to cost them all dearly. Today of all days he had ridden off and was somewhere dozing in the sun while the horses grazed unguarded. She would scold him, if her mother would not. He was supposed to be learning the ways of manhood. Sleeping instead of keeping watch was boyish enough, wasn't it? Any boy of six grasses could manage that. Jean-Paul had ten.

Celou scanned the mountainside above, the rocks that were flat enough to lie on comfortably, the rim of the clearing. "*Jean-Paul!*" she called. But there was no answer. She called again, louder. Then again. She clenched her fists, beginning to understand, feeling the fear hardening in her stomach again. Jean-Paul was not sleeping. His friends had ridden past, perhaps. Or maybe he had arranged to meet them close to the big camp to play at their boyish wars. He was not guarding the horses. He was nowhere near.

The roan whickered quietly as she came close enough to touch his neck. He lowered his head for her to rub his ears, blowing a soft grass-sweet scent into Mu'mbič's face as he did. Celou felt her brother wriggle, then heard him laugh quietly.

Using the knife awkwardly, Celou cut a strip of leather from the hem of her shift. It was crooked, wide in places and narrow in others, but she managed it, her hands shaking with urgency.

The roan stood still while she slit the leather strap at one end and pulled the other through the cut. Celou slipped the circle of leather into the roan's mouth, passing it through the gap between his molars. Leading him up to a rock, she got on, feeling the strange tug of the cradleboard's weight. Her mother always rode with Mu'mbič on her back or dangling from her saddle. Celou leaned forward, then back, then to each side, judging the difference in her balance. The cradleboard would make her clumsy. It didn't matter. It *couldn't* matter. She had to ride fast.

CHAPTER FOUR

Celou turned the roan and got the other horses moving. Slapping her leg to make a popping sound like a whip, she drove them down into the trees where they would be harder to find, at least until they wandered back up to the thicker grass in the meadow. Celou stopped, waiting a moment until they had begun to graze again.

She turned the roan slowly away and let him walk a few paces, then eased him forward into an ambling jog. One of the grays looked up, nickering questioningly. Celou hoped the horses would stay here. The roan often took the lead going to pasture and coming home. They were used to following him. Celou reined the roan in, reconsidering. Maybe she should drive all the horses ahead of her, move them so that the Crow couldn't steal them.

Celou heard a shout from below and dug her heels into the roan's sides, urging him into a trot.

There was no time. If the Crow warriors found the horses and stole them, so be it. Her job now was not to save the horses—it was to get help from her mother's family in the big camp. Having a band of horses galloping along in front of her would slow her down and make her too easy to see and hear—and track. Celou knew her father would care far less for the horses than for Bī'a's safety.

Celou glanced back. Her little mare had gone back to grazing, working her way down into the trees. So had the grays and her mother's black mare. Celou pushed her heels into the roan's sides and felt him rise into his even, light-footed canter. The unaccustomed weight of the cradleboard pulled her backward and she had to grab at the roan's mane to steady herself.

She rode as fast as she dared across the rocky hillside, turning to follow a game trail that led downward toward the creek. Mu'mbič was quiet again, and after a few minutes, Celou was pretty sure he had fallen asleep. He was used to riding like this, and the motion often lulled him. He would be really hungry in a few hours, though, she knew. And then what would she do? He would eat whatever meat she chewed up for him, but he would want to nurse as well.

Celou felt her throat constrict and she blinked

back tears. How would they manage without her mother? They would end up having to live in the big camp when Papa was off trapping or trading . . . Celou stopped the rush of ugly thoughts. Her mother needed her to be brave—not to grieve before anyone had died. With luck, Celou knew she would be able to get to the big camp, to her mother's family. They would help if she could only reach them in time.

Celou found a place to leave the game trail and urged the roan slantwise across the broad slope of the mountain. It would be smartest to ride a crooked path to the big camp—not to make a beeline.

When Celou came to a creek, she crossed halfway, then guided the roan in a splashing trot straight down the streambed for a ways, to make their trail at least a little harder to follow. On the far side, the ground was choked with gooseberry bushes. This late in the year, they had already been picked clean by women from the big camp. Celou slowed the roan to a walk again, looking for the tracks of the pickers. If they had ridden horses on their picking parties, their tracks would help conceal her own as she headed toward the camp.

A tiny sound caught her attention and at first she thought it was Mu'mbič, talking to himself the way he sometimes did. But it was not. It was muted with distance, but it was a man's voice—a shout barely audible through the stands of pines.

Celou twisted around on the roan's back, trying to pinpoint the direction. There. Above her—back toward the meadow. The Crow. Was her mother with them? Was she all right? Maybe they would just take the horses and run. Or were they tracking the roan, trying to stop her from getting help? Celou imagined them catching up with her, pulling her from the roan, Mu'mbič's cradleboard strapped to her back . . . falling. . . .

Celou forced the thoughts away angrily. She needed to be wily and smart now, like the heroes in Papa's stories. If the Crow warriors were having trouble following her tracks, they might just split up to be sure of catching her—two to follow and two to go straight down the mountain, to wait below for her to come out of the trees to cross the big meadow where the tipi stood. They would know where she was going, and they would know they had to hurry. Her mother had made the big camp sound very near, but it wasn't. It would take some time, even riding fast, to get there. She hesitated a moment longer, then turned the roan abruptly, splashing back into the little creek.

This time, Celou stayed in the water for a long

ways, holding the roan to the center where the current was strongest, most likely to wash away his swirling, muddy hoofprints fast enough to conceal them from the Crow. The little creek was overgrown with trees, the pines sometimes crooked, leaning low where the bank had washed away from beneath them. In some places she had to lie flat on the roan's back, the cradleboard tipped forward so far she could feel Mu'mbič's cheek on her neck, his warm breath on her skin.

Celou was thinking about turning the roan back to solid ground when a fallen tree made the decision for her. Massive, stretching from one bank to the other, it was too low for the roan to pass under, and too high for him to try to jump. Celou guided him up the bank, her legs tight against his sides, one hand on his mane.

The roan was light-footed. Still, he broke some stems, crushed some of the ferns. Water streamed from his sides and belly, wetting the bruised bushes and grass, leaving a clear trail to follow as they left the creek.

Celou looked behind herself twice, then she faced forward resolutely. They would either follow the direction she had been headed, believing the berry pickers' trail would be her choice as it led back to camp, or they would follow the creek and find her soon. The roan might be able to outrun their horses if he was given enough of a start. And, if they were misled for a while longer, he would. She would soon hit the open meadow where her father's tipi stood, proud and well tended and familiar. She would have to race past it, and onward, for help.

Celou tightened her legs on the roan's sides again and leaned forward, urging him to pick his way downslope through the rocks and brush as fast as he could. Mu'mbič crooned quietly and Celou did not shush him. He had been brave. Braver than many boys much older than he.

When the roan brought them down the last of the steep slope he broke into a gallop on his own. Like any good horse, he could feel her urgency and fear and knew that his speed was needed. Celou headed toward the back side of the tipi and was going to gallop straight past on her way to the camp trail.

But a form in the grass caught her eye and she reined in. Jean-Paul? It was. He was lying in the dust just outside the tipi door flap. Veering the roan to the far side of the tipi, where the Crow could not see him from the slope above, Celou felt a fever of fear threatening to rise and overcome her. She gulped in deep breaths and slid to the ground, trusting the

Celou Sudden Shout   43

roan to stand as her father had taught him. She ran around the side of the tipi as fast as the awkward cradleboard would allow.

"Jean-Paul? Jean-Paul!" she whispered as she ran, remembering the need for quiet.

He did not answer.

Mu'mbič began a small uneasy whimpering at the new jarring of his cradleboard. Celou dropped to her knees beside her brother. There was a little blood on the side of his head. When she turned him over, he groaned without opening his eyes.

Celou looked around wildly. She had to get him into the tipi. Out here, he was in danger of any passing wolf or bear, or much more likely—a coyote that smelled his blood and saw he was not moving. Celou half stood, sliding her hand beneath her brother's shoulders, gripping a handful of his soft buckskin shirt.

Backing up one small step at a time, conscious of poor Mu'mbič's nearly upside-down position, she pulled Jean-Paul to the tipi door. Pulling the willow-stick fasteners out of their slits, she undid the tipi cover and threw it wide. With nothing in the way, she dragged her brother inside.

Shrugging the cradleboard off her back, Celou laid it carefully on her own pallet. Then she managed to get Jean-Paul onto his buffalo robe. He curled into a ball and then lay still. She stood up, frantic with indecision. Mu'mbič fussed and she found dried meat for him to taste. He quieted instantly and she chewed another bite, feeding it to him with her fingers. Time grated past, scraping at her nerves. She listened for the sound of hoofbeats, of distant shouts.

"Jean-Paul!" she whispered, lifting a gourd of water to sprinkle his face. He moaned and straightened out on the robes, but his eyes remained closed. An awful lump had risen on the side of his face, and there was blood matted in his hair. Maybe he had heard the Crow warriors whooping and had come down from the meadow to try to rescue them. Celou felt ashamed of her angry thoughts. Her brother had been brave enough to face four Crow— four grown men. What had he done? Ridden toward them waving his knife? He had only his knife and a small bow, and he was really still just a child.

Mu'mbič made a sucking sound with his lips and Celou smiled at him. "More to eat, de:'për?" she asked, giving him another bit of the chewed-up meat. At least Jean-Paul was breathing easily. There was another bruise on his thigh, she noticed, but he was not bleeding anywhere. The Crow had probably spared him for his courage.

Celou gave the last of the meat to Mu'mbič,

glancing nervously out the opened front of the tipi. She had to go. Now. But should she take her brothers with her? Could she? Jean-Paul could lie across the roan's back and she could lead him along with the cradleboard on her back. But it would be so slow . . . she would never make it to the big camp before the Crow warriors found her.

"If," she said aloud, "they are even still looking for me. Once they found the horses, they might have ridden for home."

Celou blinked, shifting her weight from one foot to the other. There was no good choice. She brushed her lips across Mu'mbič's cheek, whispering to him of bravery and silence. Then she kissed Jean-Paul lightly. She said a prayer to her father's god. Finally, hanging the cradleboard as high as she could, well out of reach of wolves or snakes, she sang a medicine song she had made up while she was burying her lost teeth beneath a wild rosebush. She had not sung it since, so perhaps it would still have its whole force. She bent over Jean-Paul as she sang.

Celou stepped back once the song was finished. Her father said such things were nonsense. But then, her mother said the Christian God was a silly story. Papa prayed often, saying that God sent strength to those who asked for it. Bī'a went to the medicine men and women in the big camp when one of her family was ill or hurt.

Celou glanced back at her brothers, one unconscious and the other swinging gently back and forth in his cradleboard, then she went out. She hurried, replacing the willow fasteners and sliding the door flap back over the opening. The roan nickered when he saw her coming, his head up and his ears pricked forward. He was listening.

CHAPTER FIVE

Celou slowed her step, watching the roan. He lifted his head a little higher, pulling in big draughts of air. He scented something. Or maybe the wind was just now bringing him news of the Crow warriors. He had been a warhorse. He knew the smell of paint, the sounds of war cries. She swung up and felt the tension in his back, like a drawn bow. She touched his sides with her heels, and he sprang into a gallop that very nearly unseated her. Pounding over the ground, his mane flying back across her legs, the big roan made the meadow fly past beneath them.

At the bottom of the clearing, where the timber thickened, Celou hauled back on the single rein. The roan tossed his head, fighting the pressure, reluctant to slow down. His eyes were edged in white, and she knew he was sure they were galloping to battle. He was waiting for the first war shout, for the scent of blood. It made no sense at all to him to stop.

Celou pulled him into a circle, tightening the rein until he had to slow. Looking back toward the tipi, she realized this was about where her mother had been run down by the Crow warriors. Once Celou had the roan under control, she let him canter toward the stand of trees where her mother had tried to escape.

Celou reined in as the pines thickened. Slowing the roan to a trot, she let him pick his way downhill through the trees. Her decision now was nearly the same as it had been when she was on foot. It'd be faster to skirt the stands of pines and aspens, but then she would be easy to see from above. Maybe the Crow wouldn't come back once they had found the horses, but she couldn't be sure. They might not even realize she existed. But if they saw her now, they would probably try to cut her off before she could get to the big camp for help.

Celou ducked beneath a low limb as the roan made his way downward. Bent over his neck, she saw a glimpse of blue. It was a strip of cloth, quivering in the breeze, pierced and held by the rough thorns of a wild rosebush. Celou knew the color, knew where it had come from. It had been torn from her mother's skirt.

She reined in and stared at a jagged stump behind the bush, then up at a lightning-struck tree to one side of it. She knew this rosebush. This was where she had buried her lost teeth the year before, for luck and for a long life, and had made up her medicine song. Celou slid to the ground and picked the cloth out of the thorns. This was where her mother had struggled. This was where they had caught up with her.

Celou looked back, measuring the distance to the top of the slope. Her mother had run an incredible race, staying ahead of their horses this far. Celou fingered the cloth, leaning to look at the scuffed prints on the ground. Something beneath the bush caught her eye, and she bent to see.

It was white, too white to be anything but bone or the white stone that showed above ground on parts of the mountain, peeking through the russet of the pine needles. But the shape was odd.

Looking around quickly to make sure no one was near, Celou stooped to reach back beneath the rosebush, unable to believe her eyes. Attached to a rawhide thong was a piece of antelope hide, cured white as was the Crow custom, folded tightly into a little packet.

Celou held it in her open palm, afraid to close her fingers over it. This was a bah-park. One of the

Crow had lost his medicine. Warriors of most tribes had medicine bundles of some kind, but the Crow valued theirs more highly than anything they owned. The warrior would feel defenseless; he would be afraid to fight without his power, his bah-park.

Celou stood quickly. No warrior would leave the place where his medicine had been lost. He would be back to look for it as soon as he realized that it had fallen from his neck or his wrist—wherever he wore it.

Celou scrambled back onto the roan's back, the bah-park dangling from her hand. The warrior had probably paid dearly for the shell or stone or piece of bone that was wrapped inside the bundle. Sometimes three or four horses were paid for a good bah-park from an older warrior. If the young warrior who bought this one came home with four stolen horses and a captive, he would consider the price well spent—and be even more determined to find the bah-park once he noticed it was missing.

Celou tied the bah-park to her belt beside the knife. She pulled the roan around, backtracking exactly the way she had come, anxiously watching the mountainside above the wide meadow. The Crow's horses had left a tangle of tracks here, too, gouging the soil as they had maneuvered, trying to catch Bī'a. The roan's hooves were not so much bigger or smaller that the Crow warrior would notice when he retraced his path to look for his bah-park. He would be worried, hurrying. He might very well ride for speed rather than go slowly enough to examine the trail.

Coming back up along the edge of the meadow, Celou watched carefully for more tracks, riding close to any she saw. After a little ways, she spied a span of prints that looked like at least six or eight horses cantering in a loose group. Jean-Paul's friends, the foolish pretend-warriors, had come up from the big camp this way many times. She followed their path, hoping the Crow warriors would not pick out a single, newer track running the wrong way—until it was too late.

Celou's heart felt suddenly light with hope. If the Crow waited for their friend while he searched for his bah-park, she had a chance of getting help while they were nearby. Her mother would be rescued before the sun disappeared for the night. Her captors might get no farther than the clearing where they had overpowered her. If Mu'mbič would stay quiet a little longer, if Jean-Paul did nothing to make them ride back close to the tipi. . . .

Celou forced herself to concentrate on riding. Once she was far enough away from the tipi that the Crow warriors could not spot her, she let the roan have his head and stuck to the clearer ground above the creek. He was glad to gallop flat out. Celou rode high on his back, stretching her weight forward over his neck the way her father had taught her, helping him race along. Twice he gathered himself to jump fallen pine trunks, landing steadily and going on without stumbling. Celou whispered praises in his ear as she kept her eyes on the ground in front of them.

Near the fork in the creek, Celou veered the galloping roan onto the faint path that had been worn by Jean-Paul's friends and other visitors from the big camp. There was a small chance that she would see someone—she would be happy to see some of Jean-Paul's friends now. But the trail was empty as the roan pounded along it, following the course of the stream for a ways, then turning upward again.

Along the top of a ridge, where the path widened before it disappeared on the rocky slope of the next little valley, Celou's thoughts were shattered by a strong smell of smoke. There was always a faint smell of campfires and roasting meat, but this was strange smoke. It was sickly sweet, not like cookfires, but like burning waste or wet grass.

Celou had been watching the ground in front

of the roan. Now she looked up and scanned the horizon, confused and startled. There, rising from the direction of the big camp, was a haze of blackish smoke. Celou rode closer, staring.

Finally, topping the last ridge, she heard faint war cries that knifed through the thick, smoky air. Stunned, Celou pulled the roan to a reluctant canter, then fought him to a trot, blinking, trying not to cry out. The camp had been attacked.

Celou spotted a rocky overlook off to the west, and she rode for it, cantering out on the highest point. She could see the warriors now, riding in full battle dress, their faces painted red and yellow and white. *Blackfoot.*

The muted pop of gunfire came to her ears and she flinched. The roan pawed at the dirt, shaking his mane, but she held him in. There was nothing she could do to help her mother's people now. And there was nothing they could do to help her.

Celou heard the squealing of a terrified horse as she turned the roan in a quick circle, allowing him to dance, then rear, but keeping him reined in. He sidled and ducked his head, trying to free himself from the pressure on the rein.

Sadly, she watched the shifting scene below. In and out of the smoke she saw people running, shouting, and screaming. There was more gunfire.

A riderless horse loped out of the big camp and started south, its saddle pulled sideways, its rein dragging the dirt.

Celou squeezed her eyes closed. She could not ride through a battle to ask for help that no one could give. She was on her own.

CHAPTER SIX

Celou started the roan back up the mountain. He was less willing to gallop away from the battle, but he obeyed her and carried her over the rough ground a second time, then back along the creek. At the edge of the tipi clearing, Celou reined in and slid off his back.

She patted his neck and loosened the rein, backing away from him so he would know that she meant him to stay. She stood a better chance of remaining unseen if she were on foot. The roan's nostrils were flared, his breathing labored, and Celou could only hope that no one was close enough to hear.

Making her way from one tree to the next, Celou kept her eyes moving. If the Crow warriors were gone, she could cut across the clearing to the tipi. Perhaps Jean-Paul would be awake. She could feed Mu'mbič a little more and think about what she should do next. She ached to see her brothers, to know that they were all right. Then she would be able to think about how she could help her mother. But if the Crow warriors had not left yet, she—

A shout startled Celou's thoughts into stillness. Swallowing hard, she stopped and crouched low, creeping forward after a few seconds for a better view. At first she saw nothing, then she saw what she most feared. The Crow warriors were back near the tipi. As she watched, two of them circled it, whooping and screaming war cries. She held herself still, repeating her song, then her father's God's prayer. Then she touched the bah-park, wondering if its medicine would now work for her.

As she watched, one of the warriors pulled his mount to a halt and leapt off. He threw back the door flap and disappeared inside the tipi. Celou bit her lip, fighting tears. She had been stupid and wrong to leave Mu'mbič and Jean-Paul alone. She should have hidden them in the woods, at least, or lifted Jean-Paul onto the roan and led him . . .

"And it would have done no good," she whispered to herself. "They would have caught up to us. The camp would be no help and they would then have taken us all." Or killed us all, she allowed herself to think, feeling a shudder of fear go through her whole body. It was true. Captives were often killed.

After a moment, the warrior came back out, carrying Mu'mbič, holding the cradleboard high above his head. Celou braced herself, expecting the worst at any second. Instead, one of the other warriors urged his horse out from behind the tipi.

It was not Red-fringe, but another man who had her mother on his horse now. She was leaning out to reach for Mu'mbič's cradleboard. The Crow warrior who rode in front of her maneuvered his horse closer so she could take Mu'mbič into her arms.

Celou pulled in a long breath, then let it out. Sometimes the Crow tribe adopted captives to replace people they had lost in battle. Celou remembered the smoke rising from the big camp. She allowed herself to wonder which of Jean-Paul's friends, which of her own uncles or aunts were no more. There would be cries of grief ringing from the mountainside by tonight. Many women would cut their hair and slash their legs.

Celou watched her mother hold Mu'mbič close. The rider in front of her seemed not to notice the bulky cradleboard that must have bumped him from behind until her mother managed to slip it onto her back. Celou tried to calm her fear, but it was impossible.

Late at night, when the campfires had burned down to glowing coals, her uncles and cousins had all told tales of Crow cruelty and torture, to make each other shiver and tiptoe off to bed listening for the nearly inaudible snap of a stepped-on twig.

A shout from the far side of the clearing broke into Celou's thoughts again and she stiffened, waiting. It was a man's voice—anguished, astonished—angry. Instinctively, she moved back toward the roan, watching as she crept away.

The fourth Crow had appeared from the trees on the other side of the clearing, and Celou recognized him at once. Now he was galloping wildly, the long fringe on his sleeves streaming out in the wind as he thundered toward the two warriors near the tipi. He kept shouting, his voice harsh and insistent. In one hand he held his horse's rein tightly. His other hand was at his throat, his fingers splayed across his shirt. He had missed his bah-park at last.

Glancing back once more as she grabbed the roan's rein and scrambled onto his back, Celou saw the fourth warrior come into sight, driving her family's horses ahead of him, her mother's black mare in the lead. Under the cover of their noise, it would be impossible for the Crow to hear the roan's hoof-beats. She dug her heels into his sides and threw her weight forward. He reacted so quickly that his lunge unbalanced her and she had to grab at his mane to regain her balance.

As the roan leveled out, finding his stride, Celou glanced backward. They hadn't seen her yet, she was sure. Nor would they, if she was fast enough. She pulled the roan westward, realizing for the first time that it was almost midday now. The morning had gone.

Following the game trail for a ways, Celou added one more set of tracks to the already confusing pattern. Where the brush was thickest, she veered off the trail and continued west. Finally, after she was sure that enough distance lay between her and the tipi, she swung the roan upslope again.

Riding a wide, uphill semicircle, Celou started back eastward. As she rode, she tried to form a plan in her mind, to decide what she should do. But it was impossible to think beyond keeping out of sight, eluding the Crow warriors while she followed them when they left the tipi. There wasn't anything else she could do.

Celou touched the bah-park at her waist. Would it bring her good medicine? Or bad? She was not its rightful owner. She felt a shiver work its way up her back. Her mother would say that Crow medicine might harm a Shoshone. Her father would say all the tribes' medicine was a sham.

As Celou rode, her ears and eyes alert, her thoughts roamed. What older warrior had sold the bah-park to the man who had taken her family captive? Was he a big-medicine warrior who had killed many people in battle? How many of the scalps on his legging fringes were Shoshone scalps? Or white trappers like Papa? And Jean-Paul, if he was still alive—what would become of him? Would they leave him lying in the tipi?

Celou shivered again. Thinking was only making her heart ache. She had no choice; there was only one possible plan. She had to get above them again, where she could watch without being seen. If they left Jean-Paul behind, she had to come back to cover him warmly and to put water within his reach. But then, she had to follow the Crow warriors. She had to hope her mother's family would come find Jean-Paul and care for him when they could. She had to pray there would be a time, somewhere on the trail, when she could slip into the Crow camp and free her mother and Mu'mbič.

Maybe the Crow warriors would separate to hunt. Maybe they would argue and fight among themselves. "Please, God," Celou whispered. "Make them weak and make me strong. And watch over Jean-Paul," she added, feeling as though she were being pulled apart.

She crossed one wide meadow at a canter, then slowed to work her way through the next stand of trees. At least Mu'mbič would be able to nurse now. He would be so glad to see their mother, so sure that everything would be all right now that she was back with him.

Celou came up a draw filled with wild carrot and lamb's-quarters. She reined in to let the roan take a long drink of water from a little spring fed by a rill of water spilling from beneath a boulder. When he was finished, she slid down, the insides of her legs stinging from the salt in the roan's sweat. It was drying now, leaving his coat stiff across his shoulders. She waded into the cold water, scooping up handfuls to rinse the salt from her legs, washing the dried blood from the little cuts on her feet.

A sudden crashing in the brush made her stiffen with fear, then she saw the white flash of a deer's rump as it bounded off. She remounted, feeling foolish. She would have to be more careful. If she flushed game into the sight of the Crow, they would come see what had scared it.

Celou was careful to come out of the trees well above the tipi, so that the Crow would not be able to spot her. She took the leather she had cut from her dress from the roan's mouth and used it to hobble him, tying the knots carefully so he could not pull them loose.

She patted his neck, apologizing for the indignity. "If a wolf scared you, and you ran, what would I do?" she asked, hoping he would understand her necessity. He only rubbed his broad, flat jaw against her shoulder, so hard she could barely stand up against his affectionate shoving. Then he fell to grazing, taking the short steps that the hobble would allow.

Celou envied him, her belly cramping at the thought of food. With the roan grazing peacefully behind her, she crept out of the trees and found a place where she could look down into the clearing once more. It was easy to spot three of the warriors. They were still close to the tipi. One of them had set the meat rack back up and they had started a small cookfire. She could not see her mother or brothers. Perhaps they were all inside the tipi. Beyond, and to the west, Celou could still see the roiling dark smoke of the burning camp. She was sure the Crow had seen it by now, too.

Celou traced the path her mother had run, skimming her eyes over the downward slope of the meadow. There were trees in her way, but she could see most of the way down the slope to the place where she had found the bah-park. As she stared, she was sure she saw a flash of movement.

She let her eyes take in the whole slope as her father had taught her and Jean-Paul. There. She had been right. The fourth Crow was down there, riding in circles, searching for his medicine bundle. She touched it at her waist and imagined she felt a little tickle, an odd sensation in her fingertips. Maybe it was angry that she had picked it up.

"Buckskin—and whatever is wrapped up inside it—cannot get angry," she said aloud, echoing what she knew Papa would say if he were standing beside her. She longed to have him there. Or her mother. Either one would be calm now, strong. They would know what to do.

The shadows across the meadow below her were getting a little longer. It would be passing midday soon. Celou turned away from the clearing. Maybe she could find a few berries to eat before the Crow decided to ride out.

She slid down the side of the little valley worn by the spring's creek. After searching for a while she found a gooseberry bush, but it had been stripped clean by the women of the camp. A serviceberry bush farther upslope still had some fruit on it. They were sour, but tasted good anyway, fresh and biting on her tongue.

On the way back, she crossed a narrow small game trail and saw rabbit droppings beside it. Her mouth watered at the thought of a plump rabbit. She drank again, on all fours, bending over the water like a deer to plunge her lips below the surface, sucking the water into her mouth. It was icy and it would dull her hunger. She thought wryly about the number of times she had walked past the drying rack this day without a single thought of taking meat with her.

"I expected to ride to the camp, no farther," she whispered aloud, tired of feeling weak and foolish. She had done the best she could. She could only hope it would somehow yet be good enough. She looked down into the clearing again. Two of the Crow warriors had dismounted and were standing near the door flap. Celou clenched her fists, wishing she could see inside.

If Jean-Paul had been even a few grasses older, she knew they would probably have already killed him. But he was young enough they might let him live, might think they would make a Crow of him. And he had been very brave for one so young. All that would count in his favor.

Jean-Paul still lives, Celou told herself, seeing her mother sitting on the ground near the tipi, Mu'mbič's cradleboard propped against her knee. If they had killed Jean-Paul, her mother would be wailing, fighting them with fury and teeth if no other weapon were at hand. But Bī'a was sitting quietly, her head lowered slightly, acting the part of a quiet, frightened woman. She was biding her time, Celou knew, until she thought she had a chance of making an escape with her sons. And she would be listening, Celou knew, for some sign of *her*.

"I will come," Celou whispered, wishing her mother could hear. "I will come to help you."

Celou saw the warrior who had been searching for his bah-park ride back across the clearing. He dismounted and started talking, gesturing sharply. The other Crow gathered around him. Celou saw her mother look across the clearing, then lower her head again. Celou longed to signal her, but, of course, she could not risk being seen. She was her family's only hope now, their only chance.

CHAPTER SEVEN

Three of the warriors sat near the little fire pit and began pulling meat from the rack. As they ate, the fourth man kept talking, pacing back and forth. He was shouting. Even at this distance, Celou could faintly hear his voice when the breeze shifted just so. Every time he raised his arms to gesture, the long dangling fringes on his shirt rippled and swung.

This was the man who had lost his bah-park; Celou watched him carefully. She could see tiny spots of color on his leggings when he turned sideways. Beading? Perhaps he had a wife who spent the long patient hours required to decorate his clothing. Or perhaps a sister. Celou shook her head. His family meant nothing to her. The welfare of hers certainly meant nothing to him.

The warriors seemed unwary, relaxed. Celou marveled at their obvious lack of caution. But then, why hurry? The camp was in turmoil, and they probably knew that her father would not return for days, perhaps weeks. Word of the rendezvous spread quickly. Still, it seemed incredibly careless to loll about talking and arguing within sight of the smoke of a burning camp. What if the Blackfoot found them? Had the Crow struck some bargain with them?

Celou shook her head in amazement as, below her, in front of her family's tipi, the Crow were laying out their blankets, hobbling the horses to let them loose to graze. How could they be so sure they were safe? Red-fringe remained mounted, but the others seemed completely unconcerned.

As Celou watched, one of the men began to dance a foolish dance, pretending to fight an invisible foe. He dashed forward and put his hand out to slap the front of the tipi, pretending to count coup. Then he danced back, acting like an unarmed warrior who had touched an enemy in battle, without fighting or killing him—just to prove his bravery. Advancing to touch a foe, without fighting or killing him, was even more honored than real fighting.

"But that is a tipi," Celou groused at the distant Crow. "Not an enemy. You have counted no coup here. Jean-Paul attacked all of you. He has more courage than you will ever have. I am easily as brave as you and I am only a girl. I am *braver*," she added, willing it to be true.

As Celou watched, one of the other warriors tipped something up at his lips, his head tilted back. The warrior who had been watching the horses reached out, grabbing it from him. Celou wrinkled her brow, understanding their foolishness now. They had found her father's hidden whiskey bottle.

Papa almost never drank and he rarely used whiskey for trading, even though a lot of the independent traders and trappers did. So did the British, up north. It was only the Americans who had strict rules about it, Papa said. But it seemed like no one really abided by the rules. Some Indians would not trade with anyone who did not trade whiskey. It was useful, Papa said, if you didn't drink it. He kept it for washing out wounds, or for snakebite.

Celou looked sadly toward the smoky haze hanging over the western horizon. Sometimes the confusion and crowdedness of the camp had bothered her. But at least there, the people were together for songs and dances—and for times like this. No one in camp was alone now.

Behind Celou the roan snorted softly and she turned to see him watching her. Grass hung from his velvety muzzle. He held her gaze as if he were trying to tell her something. After a long moment, she understood.

Standing, watching, imagining the worst and feeling lonely were not going to help at all. The roan was eating, resting. He would be strong when it was time for them to follow the Crow warriors. Would she?

Celou went back to the creek and took another long, cold drink. There were no more berries. She would look for wild carrot in the clearing above a little later. For now, she would see what she could manage for meat in case the Crow drank enough to sleep until the morning.

Celou pulled the knife from her belt and cut willow lathes from the thickets growing along the water's edge. She chose them carefully, about the same size as her thumb. She bent the longest one into a circle, then released it and laid all the slender sticks in a pile while she searched along the ridge for something to serve as a tie cord. She did not want to cut her dress again if she could avoid it. Back at the tipi, her mother had a parfleche filled with slim splits of yucca leaves they had gathered in the south last winter that would have worked perfectly.

Celou finally found some strong vines. She cut several long pieces, then came back. She bent the first willow back into a circle and used the vine to bind it into shape. Then she cut one shorter stick to form a rib for the top of her trap. Using a wrapping pattern her father had taught her, she bound the rib to the circle of willow. Then she began twining long grass stems, loosely, the weave just tight enough to hold a rabbit. She added another pair of ribs, then another, until the basket was a cage with one side open.

When she was finished, Celou walked to the edge of the trees again and looked down at the tipi. The Crow were playing some gambling game now. They walked like men who have drunk too much whiskey, their stance wide-footed, their arms held just a little too high to guard their balance. Papa said whiskey did great harm in tibo cities. He said it would do great harm to the tribes as well.

Celou stood staring at the warriors, then at her mother, who was still sitting on the ground, Mu'mbič's cradleboard propped against her back now. Celou could imagine him, dozing quietly, or maybe looking out at the slope behind the tipi with his big, deep eyes. Celou realized why her mother had propped the cradleboard against her back. Mu'mbič was facing away from the Crow. She did not approve of drinking or of the games men played, gambling away the things their wives made, losing their horses. Celou knew of one man who had lost his tipi in a gambling game. His poor wife had had to tan skins and sew another. It had taken her most of a summer and the autumn that followed to finish.

Three of the warriors had stretched out upon the ground, grouped together as though they were playing the hand game or perhaps throwing dice. The fourth sat his horse a little way from the camp. As Celou watched, he changed position, cantering his horse in a half circle, then pulling up to face the northwest. She saw the fringe on his sleeves swinging as he rode. Red-fringe had not drunk as much. Perhaps he had not drunk whiskey at all.

Celou clenched her fists. One guard. She wished fiercely that she were a man, grown and strong and brave. She longed to knock the guard from his horse and make the other three run, wailing, before her furious arrows. The daydream faded when her stomach rumbled. She turned back to her work.

She found a white sage shrub and gathered enough leaves to rub her hands, the basket trap, and her balance sticks until the human scent was gone and only the sharp clean smell of sage remained.

Then she walked back down to the little stream and carefully set the basket trap on the narrow game trail. She placed succulent, fresh grass beneath it. She propped the balance sticks carefully, then weighted the basket with a heavy rock. It took a few minutes to get the rock settled properly, but once it was, Celou was sure any animal trying to get at the fresh grass would upset the balance sticks and make the basket fall. Backing away, she slapped the ground with the sage bough as she went, to erase her scent.

Sighing wistfully, Celou walked upstream a ways and crossed the creek, standing long enough in the middle for her sore feet to be numbed by the cold water. Climbing out the far side, she began to scan the bank for rotten logs. It didn't take long to find what she was looking for.

Celou's mother had shown her how to find the fat white grubs that lived in the rotten wood. No Shoshone ate them by choice, not even the Shoshone farther west who ate grasshoppers and ants. But the wriggling white grubs were good, rich food and Celou knew that hunger was her enemy as much as the Crow were.

The first rotten log she turned over yielded only the little wood lice that rolled up into tiny balls when they were frightened. The second had termites in the wood but no grubs. The third log had recently been shifted by some other hunter, human or animal, and the soil beneath it had dried out—so there were no insect dwellers at all.

Beneath the fourth log, Celou found five of the long white grubs that she knew would keep her hunger at bay. She plucked them out of the soil and placed them in her mouth before she had time to think about it. They did not taste bad. They were juicy, almost like eating a camas root, almost sweet even raw like this.

Celou drank again at the stream, then went to the roan and patted him before she walked back to the rim. Her mother was still sitting quietly. The three warriors remained lying on their sides, playing some sort of game. Red-fringe was still on his horse, watching the meadow.

Celou turned away and made her way uphill, to a small clearing that lay slantwise across the slope of the mountain. She could see the slender stems and white flowers of the wild carrot. Her father's name for this plant was Queen Anne's Lace. He had explained that the flowers were delicate, like the lace on a queen's gown.

Celou had asked him to describe lace many times, and every time, he failed to make her understand. Lace. It was something she wanted to see one day, like the stacks of blankets and hatchets and cans of coffee on the St. Louis docks. She knew her father's stories by heart. The goods were brought from St. Louis in keelboats that men hauled up the river with ropes.

Celou's stomach clenched again as she saw dozens of wild carrots along one side of the clearing where the soil was a little damper in the shade of a thick stand of aspen trees. She ran at the plants as though they might try to escape her. Using the knife to loosen the long roots, she soon had as many as she could eat. She started back down, stopping at the creek to wash the sand and soil from the white, fragrant roots.

Walking back toward the roan, she bit off the end of one of the wild carrots and began chewing the pungent white marrow. It tasted delicious. She was on her second one when she came into sight of the roan. His head was up, his ears pricked forward and he was facing the rim. Celou ran the last few steps and went past him, to look down at her family's tipi.

The Crow were mounting up. Her mother was already behind Red-fringe, Mu'mbič's cradleboard on her back now. Celou blinked. There were not four warriors now—but five?

His posture was so slumped that at first she didn't recognize Jean-Paul on her little bay mare. A Crow held his rein. Jean-Paul's hands were tied before him. He leaned dangerously outward as the Crow turned his horse sharply. Jean-Paul was weak.

Running to the roan, tucking the wild carrots in her belt, Celou dropped to her knees to undo the hobble. As late in the day as it was now, they might ride all night. Celou shivered. There were too many spirit people walking after dark, waiting to hurt anyone who came past them.

"It doesn't matter," Celou told herself. "You must do whatever the Crow do, and better." The roan nuzzled her cheek, and she rubbed his soft muzzle before she swung up. She kept the roan reined in, waiting for the Crow warriors to get enough of a lead so that they wouldn't see her following.

CHAPTER EIGHT

The warriors rode nearly straight north across the clearing, driving the loose horses ahead of them. One of the grays took the lead, picking the way for the rest to follow. Close to the tree line, Red-fringe shouted and gestured. The whole party veered a little to the east. The warrior leading Jean-Paul brought up the rear, Celou's mare trailing behind the Crow's horse. Celou watched her brother sway with every rise and fall of the land.

Once the Crow had crossed the clearing and had started uphill, into a rocky draw that led upward, Celou rode slowly across the face of the mountainside. She did not want to overtake them, or even come close enough to be seen. Nor did she want to be left very far behind.

Celou fingered the bah-park at her belt, trying to make a plan she thought could work. Again, she ached for her father's presence, his counsel. He could always figure things out. Celou imagined him at the rendezvous. He would be laughing, joking. He loved to eat and talk—and he liked the running races and shooting matches. They all bet on everything, of course. Papa said that men who drank always lost to men who did not. The year before he had won Bī'a's silver bracelets in a horse race.

Celou heard voices coming through the trees and reined in sharply. The roan tossed his head, flaring his nostrils, trying to smell what he could hear. Celou raised her hand to feel the whisper of the wind. It was streaming around her from behind. It would carry her scent *toward* the Crow's horses.

She felt a flash of fear. She should have gauged the wind before deciding to come up on the Crow from the north like this. Jean-Paul would not have made such a simple error, she knew. Any boy would have thought about this—but they were all taught to hunt and spent every day practicing. Celou felt foolish and angry at herself for making excuses. There would be few second chances today.

Pulling the roan abruptly off to one side, Celou cut downslope, riding as fast as she dared. He cantered steadily, his head high, his forelegs stiff against the steepness of the land. When Celou reined in again, she listened as the roan fidgeted. He steadied and shook a fly from his mane.

Celou sat, keeping still until she was positive. No voices now. It had been a stupid mistake, but perhaps she would not have to pay too dearly for it. She smiled wryly to herself. Now, having gotten away from them, she needed to catch up. But this time, she would come from straight behind them—from the south, so that her scent would not make the Crows' horses nervous. The last thing she needed was for them to start whinnying at the roan, betraying her presence to their riders.

Near the meadow where Jean-Paul had grazed the horses, Celou found the Crows' tracks. They were easy enough to follow. Nine horses made quite a trail. There were rolled stones and broken sage branches as well as the hoofprints gouged into the hillside. Celou saw a distinct print that looked like one of the horses was shod with the tibos' iron shoes. These Crow warriors had been stealing other horses, too.

Celou rode slowly for a while, content to stay well behind. There was no advantage in getting closer yet, only danger. Twice, coming over rises or around bends in the clearings, she saw them in the distance. Both times she quickly rode into the trees where she could watch without being spotted.

Even this far away, she could see Jean-Paul swaying precariously as Celou's little mare tried to match strides with the bigger horse in front of her. Jean-Paul was still weak, Celou was sure. It scared her to see him like this. He needed rest, not a rough ride with his hands bound. Celou longed to do something more than follow, but she could not.

After a few hours of riding, the Crow warriors veered eastward. Celou came up out of a valley and saw that they were heading toward a rim of mountain peaks that she had no names for. Her father would know them, but she did not. Her mother's people were at the northeastern limit of their lands in the summers. The realization that this was country she had never crossed, had never seen in her life, made her feel small and frightened. She twined her hands in the roan's mane and lay forward on his neck for a second, inhaling his sweet, grass odor. The roan shook his mane to rid himself of her tickling and Celou straightened up, embarrassed. She looked back over her shoulder. What would Papa think if he came home this evening to find the meadow empty and a tangle of tracks around his door? What would he do?

Celou stiffened. "I should have written him a message," Celou whispered to the roan. He flicked an ear backward, then shook his mane again. "I could have told him what happened, that I was following the Crow."

Celou was furious with herself—but only for a moment. What if she had lost them trying to leave Papa a letter—and then he hadn't come home for two or three weeks. It was possible.

Celou fingered the hilt of the knife in her belt. Maybe she should cut marks into trees as she passed or leave some other kind of trail. She remembered her father talking about men who devised marks to be left on trees that meant something about how far water was, the condition of the grass. But she knew no such marks.

As she thought it her eye fell on a big dark-colored rock with one flat side. She turned the roan toward it and slid off, running the last few steps. She pulled the knife from her belt and tried scraping at the rock. The knife tip left a streak on the rock surface. If she scratched it back and forth a little, the mark was noticeable from a little ways away.

Celou set to work. *Papa*, she wrote. The letters were clumsy and crooked, but she was pretty sure he could read it, if he saw it. But then she hesitated. She tried to think of a way to write what had happened without needing eight or ten big rocks and a week's time. But she couldn't. Finally, glancing up every few seconds to make sure the Crow had not seen her, she set to work again.

She drew little four-legged figures with two-legged figures astride them. She drew five of them, with two riders and the arch of a cradleboard on one and a slumping figure, smaller than the other riders, on the last one. Then she drew four horses without riders. Lower on the rock, by itself, she drew one last horse, a big one, with a small rider: herself.

When she was finished, Celou stepped back and looked at the drawing. If Papa looked at it closely, he might understand what she was trying to tell him. Celou glanced around. If Papa or her mother's family came this way, there was nothing to ensure that they would even notice the rock. If they rode even a slightly different path, they could easily miss it.

Celou pulled the strip of blue broadcloth from her belt and laid it on top of the flat-sided boulder, draping it downward so that it hung across the drawings themselves. She weighted it with a smaller stone, then stood back again.

There. Someone would have to be half asleep to miss the unnatural blue of the cloth. Celou got back up on the roan. She let him settle into a ground-covering trot. Her stop had widened the distance between her and her family.

Celou followed the tracks for a long time before she caught another glimpse of the Crow warriors.

When she did, she slowed, letting the roan drink at the next creek and graze a little. She wanted him to rest when he could. She might need every bit of his strength before her family was safe again—if they ever were.

CHAPTER NINE

As the afternoon mosquitoes began to whine and buzz around her ears, Celou kept looking at the bah-park tied to her waist. It was her only power over Red-fringe and his friends. And if they caught her, they could take it so easily.

All around Celou the countryside rose and fell, stretching away toward the sky. There were as many rocks as stars and there were trees without number. Many of them would give good hiding places.

Celou rode slowly, glancing at the trail before her, then staring off to both sides, thinking hard. The rocks here were whiter than those lower on the slope and smoother, too, almost like the white stone knives the Tosawis sometimes traded to her father.

Celou began to look for a landmark, a place keeper—and she began to form a plan in her mind. If she ended up back here, it would be in the company of Red-fringe, and perhaps his friends.

She had to choose a hiding place carefully.

As she passed a huge white boulder split along its top, she abruptly turned aside, leaving the Crow's trail of hoofprints. She rode a little ways, straight into the trees. These were aspens, tall and perfect for her purpose.

Celou stopped within a thick stand of aspen, their soft white trunks scarred with ash gray wherever a limb had grown or where the bark had been bruised. One set of four horizontal scars caught Celou's eye. A bear tree. The marks were from a male bear, standing to his full height to slash at the trunk with his claws.

Celou stared at the marks. The Bu'ha-gant in her mother's tribe who attended difficult births had bear medicine. Bī'a said bear medicine was strong because bears were so powerful. Celou lifted her right leg over and sat sideways on the roan's back, then slid off.

She stood, stretching her cramped muscles before she began to stare up into the branches. She wanted a tree with high limbs strong enough to allow a girl to climb them—but not a man.

Celou pulled the knife from her belt and walked back through the trees to the Crows' trail in the clearing. Low, near the soil line, she marked a tall aspen, cutting a V shape in the bark. Then she rolled a white stone near it, placing a fallen pinecone atop the stone. A casual rider would go right past, but she would know this was the exact place to turn aside.

Celou hurried back to the bear tree. She didn't want to fall too far behind the Crow, especially now, when they would be likely to make camp soon—or at least she hoped they would. Wincing at the bruises on her legs and the cuts on her feet, she shinnied up the smooth-barked trunk. Using the side branches to brace her feet and as handholds, she climbed as high as she could, without stopping or looking back down. Then, slowly, she worked her way out onto one of the topmost limbs. As she had known it would, it began to bend beneath her weight. She edged a little farther, determined to hide the bah-park in the most difficult place she could.

Careful of her balance upon the sagging limb, Celou pulled the Crow's medicine bundle from her belt and used its thongs to tie it tightly to the branch. She tied hard knots her father had taught her, trapper's knots, one atop the other. Then, when she was sure the thongs could not slip or loosen, she climbed down.

It took Celou a little while to catch up to the

Crows again. She got as close as she dared, catching a glimpse of their distant figures once in a while on the mountainside ahead of her. As the day neared its end, she kept careful watch, alert for any movement that would tell her one of the Crow warriors was riding back down the trail to make sure no one was following them. Papa always did, especially if they had met anyone along the way who made him cautious.

As the afternoon went on, the Crow seemed to be slowing down. Even riding at an easy pace, Celou found herself gaining on them, once coming dangerously close to being seen. She dropped back, then slowly went on. A little later, she saw something.

The flash of movement in the trees was so quick she could not be sure if the rider was headed away from her or toward her. To be cautious, she slowed even more, then stopped in the deepest shadows she could find. She held the roan still, waiting.

After a time, she heard hoofbeats, the steady clopping of a horse trotting at a moderate pace down the mountainside. The roan lifted his head and Celou leaned forward to tap his jaw with her fist. "No sound," she whispered to him. "No whinnying."

His neck straightened a little, the arch flattening as he lowered his head. She patted him. He was a good horse, a good companion in danger. The hoofbeats came closer.

Celou leaned forward, peering through the trees, trying to see the rider. When she finally did, she held her breath. He was going to pass by closer than she had thought. She could see the yellow paint around his eyes, blending into the red that covered the rest of his face. She lay flat on the roan's neck and waited.

The hoofbeats came nearer still, the Crow's horse keeping its pace steady in spite of the rocks and the slope. Celou watched him ride past, close enough that she could see his eyes flickering back and forth over the forest for an instant between the trees. It was Red-fringe, on his tall bay.

The forest is thick, Celou told herself. *The shadows are deep. If there is no sound to direct his eyes, he will not discover me.*

The sudden slowing of the hoofbeats startled Celou. Then there was silence. The warrior had pulled his horse to a stop. Celou held very still, willing the roan not to stamp away a fly or flutter a breath to blow a gnat from his nostrils. Any sound at all could bring the warrior galloping after her. She could not see him now, but he was still dangerously close. She heard hoofbeats again. There he was. Between two tree trunks, he came into view, then stopped once more. Celou's mouth went dry.

Red-fringe sat his horse easily, his legs relaxed, his posture proud. He looked fierce, angry. Celou lowered her head as he turned and seemed to look right at her. Then his eyes drifted onward and he twisted the other way, looking, listening. Celou saw his right hand touch the base of his throat.

Abruptly, the Crow warrior turned his mount back upslope, but then, just as suddenly, he reined in again. The horse tossed its head and stamped one hind hoof, striking a rock. The sharp ringing of iron on stone startled Celou. His horse was *shod*. That meant it had recently been a white man's horse.

Celou could feel her hands trembling, and she lifted them from the roan's neck so her fear would not make him uneasy. He flicked his ears back, then forward again.

As Celou watched, the warrior yawned. He lifted his bow and pretended to take aim at a songbird that flew overhead, then lowered it again. He turned his mount downslope once more, and Celou felt her heartbeat quicken. If he rode past her and went on downhill, he might notice the roan's tracks, mixed in with the others crisscrossing the slope. He paused again, tilting his head, listening. Celou forced herself to breathe evenly, silently. She bit her lip, fighting the incredible pressure of her own fear.

Abruptly, the warrior sat up straighter, as though a sudden thought had struck him. He turned his horse uphill and touched his heels to its sides, urging it back into a trot. Celou watched him through the trees, a few flashes of red paint, a glimpse of the dark bay horse. She caught one last image of his fierce, menacing face as he passed between two tall pines, then angled away from her. Then, finally, he was gone.

Celou stroked the roan's neck and was surprised to feel the sweat beneath his smooth coat. He had been nervous, too. She was shaking, trembling with the urge to wheel the roan around and gallop away. As if he had felt her impulse, he shook his head, letting his mane whip back and forth, stinging Celou's hands and wrists. He lowered his head and nosed at the ground. Celou pulled in a deep breath, then let it out slowly, willing herself to calm down. She had to. Before this night had ended she would probably have to come much closer to the Crow warriors than this.

She slid to the ground and stood on her unsteady legs for a moment before she dared take a step. Patting the roan and dropping his rein to ground-tie him, she worked her way to the edge of the stand of trees. She shaded her eyes against the slanting sun and then squinted to make her vision reach farther. He was gone. He truly was gone now. Celou allowed herself to slump against the trunk of an aspen.

Celou knew she had to move closer to the Crow now. She needed to see the Crow camp while it was still light enough for her to learn where her mother was going to sleep with Mu'mbič and where Jean-Paul would be allowed to rest for the night.

"And Red-fringe," she whispered to herself as she started back toward the roan.

As Celou rode, still tensely alert like a deer that scents a mountain lion, the sun was getting lower in the sky. The tracks led nearly straight west now, across a high saddle of land just below timberline. As the trees got sparser, Celou rode carefully, sometimes dismounting and leaving the roan long enough to creep forward and make sure that the next meadow was empty before she went on.

The Crow had speeded up again. They had not stopped to rest or eat, Celou was sure. She watched the tracks, seeing, more than once, the kicked-up clods of soil that meant a horse had been urged into a sudden canter, then pulled back in after a few strides as the ground got rocky or too steep. They were in a hurry now, it seemed; they had probably wasted too much time drinking her father's whiskey and now were afraid they wouldn't get as far as they wanted by nightfall.

As she rode upslope, there were fewer and fewer trees. Celou could only hope Red-fringe was satisfied no one was following them. If he rode back down their trail now, there would be nowhere for her to hide. Where the grass thinned out and much of the soil was bare, Celou could pick out the tracks of her own mare—the smallest hoof of the group and the lightest step. As she had all day, she looked for signs of her family, any evidence that they had been allowed to dismount to relieve themselves or to drink at any of the icy creeks she crossed—but there was none.

The Crow warriors had not dismounted anywhere either, as far as she was able to tell. They were riding like a war party now, swift and straight. Coming up a steep rise, unable to see beyond the top of it, Celou reined in and glanced around for cover. Then, as she had done several times before, she rode the roan at a gallop toward the nearest trees, slid off and left him there while she edged back out into the open.

She angled across the slope, dodging from one boulder to another, then crawling on all fours in the thickest grass she could find. She came to the top of the ridge and looked downward, expecting an empty meadow like all the others she had ridden through since morning. But this meadow was not empty.

CHAPTER TEN

Celou lowered herself flat onto the ground. Peeking through the grass, she lay rigid, scared. She had been expecting, for an hour or more, to see the warriors stopping for the night, making a hasty camp. She had been *hoping* they would not go on much longer, for Jean-Paul's sake. But this was not what she had hoped for at all. What she saw brought tears stinging into her eyes.

The meadow held twelve brush lodges, the kind people made when they were traveling fast. At the center of the lodges, Celou could see her family's horses, bunched together as two women looked them over. Celou scanned the rest of the clearing.

She could not see Bī'a or her brothers. Had they been taken into one of the grass lodges? Celou studied the roughly made shelters. These coni-gan had been built quickly, with little thought of permanence, that much was obvious.

There were only six warriors in the clearing. But there were twenty-five or thirty women. Celou squinted, thinking. They were probably following a much larger hunting party, these six warriors charged with protecting the women as they traveled.

A flash of blue between the lodges caught Celou's attention, and she spotted her mother. Mu'mbič was on her back, the cradleboard hanging crookedly. Celou saw her mother trying to shrug it straight—her hands were bound and the cradleboard straps had slid to one side. One of the Crow women noticed and helped her, walking on without looking back. Another, older woman stopped beside Bī'a and plucked at her dress, testing the strength of the white man's cloth.

Celou could not see Jean-Paul. Red-fringe was talking to the two older men she had never seen—whose faces had not been painted. He was gesturing, pointing back in the direction they had come. Maybe one of these men, Celou thought, had sold him his medicine. Red-fringe would be ashamed to admit he had lost it.

A whooping shout made Celou glance to the left. One of the warriors she had followed was running toward the group in the center of the camp. He pushed his way forward through the milling women until he stood facing Red-fringe.

Red-fringe embraced him and Celou wondered if they were brothers or cousin-brothers. They moved away from the others, walking side by side. As Celou watched, Red-fringe touched his throat and the younger man stopped abruptly, as though an arrow had passed close to his face. Then he shouted something in an angry voice.

Celou saw Red-fringe make a quick gesture, silencing his friend. Then he jutted out his chin and began to walk again. Celou looked past them, trying to keep track of everything that was happening.

Her mother was still standing near the horses, Mu'mbič held awkwardly in her arms now. Someone had to have helped her out of the straps. Celou watched, puzzled at her mother's sudden sinking to her knees in the grass. Then she understood. They were letting Bī'a nurse Mu'mbič. Celou watched her mother awkwardly positioning the cradleboard with her bound hands, then opening the hooks on the front of her dress.

When Bī'a finally stood again, the cradleboard acted almost as a shield, protecting her from the ring of women who had surrounded her. They were pulling at her dress, poking at the cloth and joking with each other. As her mother shifted her arms beneath the cradleboard, Celou could see rawhide strips around her wrists.

Celou caught a glimpse of Jean-Paul when the women moved aside. He had been tied to a slim-trunked aspen at the far edge of the camp. Celou winced, looking at him. His head had fallen forward, his chin on his chest. He did not move—not even to look around.

A chorus of shouts went up from the women around her mother, and Celou looked back. They were pulling hard at her dress now. Celou heard the cloth begin to tear, revealing the buckskin shift her mother wore underneath. The blue broadcloth was a fine quality most of these Crow women had probably never seen, Celou knew. Her father had paid a friend to bring it back from St. Louis.

The women were pushing Bī'a farther and farther across the clearing, separating themselves from the men. A second round of astonished women's voices rose into the air when Bī'a's bracelets were noticed. Celou stared helplessly as the Crow women wrestled Mu'mbič from her mother's arms so they could get the bracelets off her wrists.

Celou bit at her lip to keep from crying out, sure they were about to do her brother serious harm, but they only laid the cradleboard against the tree where Jean-Paul sat slumped.

It took Celou a little time to understand what they were doing, but once she did, she felt her blood heat with anger. It wasn't just the bracelets they were after. Once two women had removed the bracelets, holding tightly to one apiece, others closed in. They pulled harder at her mother's blue dress, their faces rapt with interest. They wanted to look at it, to see how it was made, and they were going to tear it off her back to satisfy their curiosity.

Celou saw her mother wrenching one way, then the other. But there were too many pairs of hands grabbing, reaching. Celou heard the sound of the tearing cloth and saw her mother whirl around, trying in vain to break their grip.

The women pressed closer, the circle shrinking until Celou caught only quick glimpses of her mother's angry face, her bound, helpless hands. Some of the women were laughing. The tearing sound began again and Celou heard her mother cry out once, then again as the seams were ripped open and the dress was finally jerked free. The Crow woman who had helped with the cradleboard held the dress above her head like a war trophy. Then she spread it out on the ground.

Celou saw her mother crawling awkwardly aside, her hands still tied, as the women gathered around the heap of blue broadcloth. She stayed low, scrabbling sideways until she was near the sapling that supported both her sons. Celou saw Jean-Paul look up as she neared and she wanted to shout for joy. He was not unconscious.

The women were laughing louder now, standing in an uneven circle around the blue dress. Celou could hear them clearly, their voices shrill and raucous. The dress was a mystery to them, Celou was sure, just as it had been to her and her mother at first. The seams were intricate and the shape of the cloth, curving inward, then outward to fit her mother's body, was strange and fascinating.

Celou wished it were dark, that she could use their interest in the dress as a chance to slip past them. But she could not. There was nothing she could do but wait. She glanced at the sinking sun. It would not be long. Perhaps an hour before dark, then another few hours to make sure the camp was asleep.

Celou looked at her mother again. "Bī'a," she whispered. "I am here. I will help. I have medicine, though I am only a girl. I found a bear tree and climbed it to the top."

Celou felt silly after she had whispered. She sounded like an imitation of Jean-Paul, with his dreams of glory and coup counting and honor in war. Still, the thought of the bear tree and her climb served to calm her a little. She had never climbed so far before. And she had managed to follow the warriors this far without them finding her. Perhaps she did have strong medicine.

A man's shout startled Celou. She looked down to see a warrior facing her way. For a fleeting and dizzy instant, she thought he had seen her. But he was pointing at something else. Something on the ground.

Celou strained to see. The man kept stepping back, quick footed and agile. Celou raised her head just a little. What was it? The Crow were forming another loose circle now, several of the women carrying pieces of her mother's dress over their shoulders. Why? Was this some kind of game?

Celou lay still, watching. She was grateful that no one had hurt her family. Captives in any camp were often tortured or killed. Her own people did these things. All the tribes did, her father said, and white men killed in their own way. There were terrible stories about trappers preying on the poor root diggers in the southern badlands, scaring them, sometimes even shooting them for no reason at all.

Celou blinked back tears. The world was a hard place, Bī'a always said, with no one ever really certain of living another sun. If she managed to free her family, Celou knew it would become a tale told by campfires—the tale of the brave girl who did the impossible. But how could she defeat six warriors? Celou lay in the grass, watching the Crow form themselves into a loose circle. Was this a hunting dance? But they were all watching the ground now.

"Aiiiihhhh!" one older woman shouted.

"Aiiiihhhh!!" another woman echoed.

They both hopped backward, staring at the earth in front of them. One of the paint-faced warriors ran across and posted himself beside them. He had a long stick and he thrust it at something in the grass. Now the far side of the circle began backing away. Two women bolted from the line and ran to a thicket above the camp. They emerged with long forked sticks.

They joined the man with a forked stick and all three began poking at the grass. The people opposite them parted, streaming to either side, opening up a clear path between the stick wielders and Celou's family.

Celou felt a sweat break out on her upper lip. Her mother was looking up, standing. She struggled to raise the cradleboard as high as she could in her bound hands. She kept glancing back at Jean-Paul who was still slouched forward, tied to the sapling.

Celou felt a cold fear seeping into her thoughts. One of the Crow warriors began shouting a single word, over and over. Red-fringe picked up the chant and the stick holders went to work again, jabbing at the grass.

Celou could not see, nor could she understand the shout, but it didn't matter. She knew what they were doing. They had found a rattlesnake, and they were going to see if the Shoshone woman and her sons had courage or not.

As Celou watched, she could measure the distance to the snake by her mother's movements. She was trying to distract it, but the stick jabbers kept it moving toward Jean-Paul. Unhampered by the broadcloth dress, her mother was quick and strong, but her hands were still tied together and she still held the cradleboard out in front of herself, the top pinched in her fingers.

Jean-Paul was alert now, straining against the rawhide bonds that held him in a sitting position. He and his friends sometimes caught rattlesnakes to prove their bravery. But pinning a snake down with a long forked stick and facing it weaponless, on its own level, were two very different things.

Celou tightened her hands into helpless fists. She said a prayer to her father's God, then asked Coyote, the father of the Shoshone, to help her mother. It was easy to see where the snake was. The stick bearers were driving it forward, then leaping back when it turned to coil and face them. Celou looked past them at her mother. She was lifting Mu'mbič's cradleboard overhead, hanging it on the stub of a limb that had probably been broken off for firewood.

Once the cradleboard was secure, Celou saw her mother start to climb the tree, slowly, clumsily, her hands pinned together by the rawhide. Jean-Paul was looking up at her as the slim trunk bent under her weight.

The Crow were shouting, laughing, a hard-edged, derisive sound. Celou blinked back tears. She understood why her mother had climbed the tree, could certainly imagine her terror at the writhing, fear-crazed snake. But trying to escape like this was only going to make things worse. A murmur in the crowd made Celou blink her tears aside. Her mother stood on the sapling's sturdiest limb and was tearing the next stoutest one free, her movements jouncing the cradleboard on the limb below. Celou heard the branch crack. Then, in one leap, her mother was back on the ground, placing her feet in a wide, solid stance. Eyes fixed on the ground in front of her, Bı̄'a stood, breathing hard. Celou saw that the stick was thick and stout as an ax handle as her mother raised it.

"Aiiiiih," the same woman shouted, as Celou's mother swung the stick downward. The Crow jumped back, several of them stumbling into people who moved more slowly.

"Ba'diiiii," her mother shouted, and Celou felt a thrill of pride and astonishment crawl up her spine. "Daughter," her mother yelled again, as though it was a war shout.

Celou watched, transfixed, as her mother raised the stick again and brought it down. This time, the snake's tail rose into the air from the impact of the blow. Her mother brought the stick up and smashed it downward a third time.

Then she stood, panting, staring at what she had done. She lifted the stick high and made as if to swing it at one of the warriors. He flinched, then she turned and threw it, as hard as she could two-handed. It spun end for end through the air over the warrior's head.

The blows had landed true. The snake lay dead. The whole circle stopped moving. Celou watched the Crow as they turned, one to the next, talking in lowered voices. She fought a desire to rise to her feet, to call out that she would try to live up to her mother's courage. She would tell Papa this story—how Bī'a had killed the snake and made the warrior flinch.

Celou lifted her head to see better. The Crow warriors were surrounding her mother now, some of them touching her lightly. She shrugged them off and reached up into the tree once more. Mu'mbič's cradleboard swinging from her hands, she sat down beside Jean-Paul. He had slumped forward again.

CHAPTER ELEVEN

Dusk, when it finally came, felt almost like a welcome warm blanket being drawn over Celou. The camp was quieting. The six warriors were gambling, standing and sitting around one of the lodges while the women began the work of preparing supper.

The warriors who had captured Celou's family had all cleaned the paint from their faces, but Redfringe was still easy to spot. Even at this distance, Celou could recognize him. He and another man rode out of camp to the west just at dusk. Celou waited, tensely. Would they separate and circle the camp? If they did, they might see the roan.

When it was almost dark, the two men returned and hobbled their horses, turning them out with the camp herd. Celou backed away from her vantage point carefully, then went and moved the roan from the trees to a grassy hollow farther down the slope. It was shielded from the camp by a thicket of wild plums.

Celou stood still, listening to the voices from the camp, hearing laughter and what sounded like an argument. No other sentries appeared. Perhaps they were confident that they had not been followed, that no one would be able to follow their trail in the dark.

Waiting for the darkness to thicken, Celou yearned for something to eat. Little ribbons of scent came on the cool, sighing breeze that slid down from the heights. Meat was cooking in the camp. She could smell the sweet odor of yampa root being dug out of last night's deep beds of coals. She heard women laugh.

Celou imagined her mother and brothers, tied up at the edge of the camp, hungry, tired, hurt. Mu'mbič had nursed, so he at least would not be hungry. But Jean-Paul would be aching and sick as well as exhausted. And her mother. . . .

"Stop," Celou whispered to herself. "Today's worries will fly at sunrise." She smiled, saying it. It was one of her father's favorite sayings. She could only hope that this time it would be true.

She nuzzled her face into the roan's side, feeling the warmth of his skin. He curved his neck, reaching around to nuzzle her shoulder. "I am afraid," Celou said into his speckled coat. "I am afraid to die."

The roan lowered his head and began to graze. Celou straightened. It was time to go watch the Crow camp, while the cookfires were high enough to light the clearing a little. She pulled in a long breath, then let it out in a rush, wishing there was some way to wait until morning. As much as the Crow warriors, the darkness scared her.

The night scared every Shoshone. So many bad things roamed in the dark. No one wanted to meet a dzō'ap with rattling skeleton bones and the power to cause terrible harm. Her mother had seen a dzō'ap once, when she was small. It was a woman skeleton, standing outside the camp, singing a sad song. Bī'a had run all the way back to her tipi.

Celou had heard her mother's story a dozen times. Her father, of course, said there were no dead people walking the earth, rattling their bones at the living. But Celou had seen the look on her mother's face as she told her tale. *She* believed it to be true. And how could she have mistaken a skeleton woman for anyone else?

Celou shook her head to free herself of such thoughts. She took a few steps in the deepening dusk, straining to see the ground. She peered into the trees and bushes she passed, half expecting to see a shadow figure, one that would leap at her, shrieking and moaning.

Celou's shoulders were hunched and tense. She heard a tiny sound, probably wood's mice, but she froze and stood rigidly, staring into the night, unable to stop expecting the rattle of bones, or a Crow war cry. Neither came. She moved forward again, placing her feet carefully.

With her next step, a rounded, snakelike shape rolled beneath her bare foot. She gasped and jumped back. The shape was still, unmoving. Frozen in place by fear, Celou stared at it for a long time in the darkness. Cautiously, she bent to pick up a pebble. She threw it at the dark shape. The pebble bounded past, making a trickling sound on the rocky soil. The dark shape did not move. Celou toed it, feeling foolish. A stick. Not a rattlesnake.

Once more, Celou started forward, walking slowly. She set each foot carefully and hesitated before taking her next step. This fear was one her father would call reasonable. The rocks would still be warm from the day's sun. Rattlesnakes were often found in pairs. The one her mother had killed might have had a companion . . . and it could be out on this warm night, crawling alone.

A bu'ha-gant who lived with her mother's people claimed to have medicine against snakebite. Her father said the old man only thought he had such medicine. Her mother had traded a pair of moccasins for a medicine bundle and had hidden it from Papa.

For a long moment, Celou missed her father so much it was painful. She wanted him to be here, beside her in the dark, unafraid. He often went outside their tipi at night and simply walked around, staring up at the stars and the moon. Bī'a always sat tense and fearful, waiting to hear his scream. When it did not come, she embraced him as he came back in, her eyes bright with relief.

Celou swallowed and forced herself to keep walking, amazed at the spinning of her thoughts. The rim of the rise seemed a hundred miles away as she went. The darkness closed itself over her body, and she could feel a clammy sheen of sweat on her lip and around her hairline.

A sighing in the pine branches above her head put a hitch in her step, and she had to force herself not to freeze. It was wind, she told herself. Only wind. "Papa says there are no ghosts, no dzõ'ap, no ogres with baskets lined with thorns," she whispered to herself. She took another step. "No water-ghost-woman. No Coyote to carry me away on his tail if I am not good."

Just walk, Celou thought, holding herself straight, her heart like a rabbit's in a basket trap, waiting for the trapper to come. The night was full of dangers, or it was not. It did not matter. She had to go on.

Celou could see the orangish glow of the campfires as she topped the ridge, and they comforted her. The camp was noisy, lit, human. As before, she crawled the last little bit of the way, keeping low. She would be silhouetted by the stars, her shape a blacker place through which no starlight fell.

Peeking through the tall grass, Celou saw four campfires, each one close to the door of a lodge. Beyond them all, dim shapes in the dark, huddled at the base of the slender tree, were her mother and her brothers. Bī'a was sitting near Jean-Paul. It was impossible to see details, but Jean-Paul looked exactly as he had for hours. He leaned to one side. Mu'mbič's cradleboard was hanging from the stubbed limb, swaying back and forth a little. He was probably asleep.

As Celou watched, her mother reached up with both hands to give the cradleboard a little nudge. Her hands were still bound. Had they bound her feet as well?

The Crow camp had quieted for the evening. Around each campfire, women sat and talked. Boiling skins hung beside two of the fires. Celou saw a woman lifting heated rocks with two sticks, dropping them into the paunch. The water within spit and hissed as the rock sank. Celou felt her mouth flood with saliva.

They would keep heating rocks and dropping them in until the water boiled. In a little while they would have stewed meat. The shifting night air brought Celou the distinct smell of the rocks, a sharp, metallic odor that blended with the scents of grass and smoke and meat.

Celou looked at her family again, then began to examine each of the faces around the campfires one by one. There. At the second fire, sitting a little apart from the women, was the man she sought: Red-fringe. He raised his arm to gesture as he spoke to a man across the fire. Rising up on her elbows, Celou fixed his face in her mind. He had a high forehead and the kind of sharp, high cheekbones that women admired. His hair was caught up in a bundle now at the nape of his neck. He had used a quill comb to gather the stray ends.

As Celou sat, the darkness pressing at her back, she found herself staring into the fires the way she would have at home, if this day had been like any other. The leaping orange flames calmed her, even at this distance, and she felt a little less afraid of the dzṓap.

Perhaps they would not come so close to a

Crow camp. Maybe Shoshone ghosts were afraid of Crow ghosts? This thought steadied her. Crow ghosts would not bother Shoshone living, she was sure. It was possible that in this one way, she was safer tonight than she had been on any other in her life. She wondered if her mother had had the same thought. She hoped so. It seemed only fair that among all these new dangers, one of the old ones would ease just a little.

Celou watched, her own stomach empty and cramping, as the Crow ate their fill, men and women sitting in rough circles around each fire. As they finished the women cleared away the mess, dropping bones into the fires and carrying their boiling skins inside to hang from a tipi pole, safe from coyotes or wolves for the night.

The men around the fires thinned rapidly once eating was finished. Women hung the boiling bags from a tree at the edge of the clearing. They burned the waste to ash, then fell into quiet talk. After a time, they stood up slowly, straightening their backs, looking up at the stars.

Celou saw her mother lying on the ground, dozing beside Jean-Paul. Red-fringe was among the last few people to go into a lodge. Celou watched him bend over, the long strips of rolled ermine skin on his sleeves brushing the ground as he ducked

Celou Sudden Shout   113

through the doorway. She was glad. At least ten or twelve people had already gone into that lodge. He would be sleeping very close to the door. If anyone heard her and her family escaping, he might be among the first to waken. And if that much went wrong, he might be their only chance.

Celou waited until the last Crow had gone back into a brush lodge before she stood up. Then, when she did, she felt strangely lonely. It was odd, as though she missed the company of the Crow now that they were gone for the night.

"You are just afraid of the dark," she told herself in a nearly silent whisper. She knew as she said it that the time for her to go down into the Crow camp was nearing. She could see the silvering of the horizon that meant the full moon was about to rise. She could wait no longer. There was no choice.

CHAPTER TWELVE

The slope above the Crow camp was steep. Celou crept down it, aware that a rolling rock, if it clattered into other stones, could wake everyone in the camp. Every step mattered, every movement had to be perfect, slow, silent. Think about anything, Celou commanded herself. Anything except what will happen if they hear you and wake up.

Above Celou's head, the sky was as black as her writing ink, with stars scattered like shattered ice. Her father always said there was no serpent up there, holding up the sky. Celou paused, gathered herself, then took the next step. But if there was no giant snake, then what did hold the sky up, Celou wondered. She blinked and paused again, fighting to make out the rocks and the clumps of grass in the darkness. Then she began to walk again.

When she finally reached the base of the slope, Celou stopped to wipe sweat from her face, even though the night air was cool this high in the mountains. At the edge of the camp, Celou paused, again staring across the clearing at her mother and brothers. Was Bī'a awake?

The sudden, high-pitched howl of a coyote startled Celou so badly that her whole body jerked, her knees bending so she hunkered down, nearly losing her footing altogether. The shrill, demented yapping racketed through the clearing, then stopped as abruptly as it had begun. Celou's heart hammered and she stayed low, waiting to see if any of the Crow would waken. If one of them saw her now . . .

The silence seemed to solidify around her, like creek water freezing around a log, holding her still. Across the clearing she saw her mother raise her head, arching her back. Then she sat up. In the same moment, there were soft stirrings inside the lodge that was closest to Celou.

Celou looked at the stars and waited for the coyote to cry out again. Maybe it wouldn't. Sometimes, they howled once, then moved on. Other times, a single howl introduced the wailing of the whole pack.

Celou waited as long as she could, grateful for every instant of silence that passed. Finally, she stood up and began her painfully slow, desperately quiet walk across the clearing. Halfway across, Celou knew that her mother had seen her. Even in the faint light of the rising moon, Celou recognized her mother's habit of leaning toward whatever she was watching. As Celou got close, she found herself smiling, and knew her mother was smiling back at her—even though it was impossible to see that clearly.

"Bī'a," Celou whispered when she could finally drop to her knees beside her mother. Her mother greeted her formally, brushing Celou's cheek with her own.

"Ba'di," she said. "Daughter. You heard me call?"

"I heard," Celou said. "Did you know I was there?"

Her mother shook her head. "I meant it to carry all the way home, to comfort you there. All of this long day I have imagined you weeping, alone and afraid at our tipi."

Celou shook her head. "All of this long day I have followed your tracks uphill, here, to this camp."

"I have nearly got one hand free," Bī'a breathed, lifting her wrists for Celou to work at the knots. "I was going to try carrying both of them." She nodded toward Jean-Paul's slumped form, then raised her eyes to the cradleboard. She leaned close to Celou's ear. "There was talk of adopting us, making us Crow." There was disgust on her face. She turned and put out her feet. They had been bound as well.

Celou realized suddenly that the moon had risen, its cold light making it possible to read her mother's expression. She loosened the last of the knots on her mother's wrists and rocked back on her heels.

There is a guard, sleeping near the horses, Celou's mother signed.

"I have Papa's roan," Celou whispered. Her hands were flying over the rawhide ropes on her mother's feet now. They were so tight that her mother's ankles had swollen. Bī'a could not stand up at first. While Bī'a rubbed life back into her legs, Celou turned to Jean-Paul.

Celou untied Jean-Paul's feet very gently, wincing when she saw the blood that had dried along his hairline. Then, her fingers over his lips so that he wouldn't cry out, she nudged him. His eyes flew open. She watched the confusion in his eyes clear as he remembered where he was and recognized her. He glanced up at Bī'a, who was rocking the cradleboard now.

Celou began working at the rawhide knots that

bound him to the sapling. Kneeling behind him, she pulled at the rawhide as hard as she could, but it had been wetted. It was hard as a rock now, stiff and unbelievably tight.

"Hold still," she whispered into Jean-Paul's ear. "I am going to use the knife." He looked at her over his shoulder and nodded, then lifted his hands a little so she could see better.

"Hurry," Celou heard her mother breathe. "Mu'mbič."

She said no more than that, but Celou heard a tiny murmur from above her head and understood her mother perfectly. Mu'mbič was hungry or perhaps wetter than he could stand. In either case, he would soon waken, and when he did, it would be very hard to keep him from making noise.

Jean-Paul was rubbing his feet and legs now. He put his hands over his face and shuddered when he touched his own bruises. "Can you run?" Celou asked him.

"I think so," he breathed. "Soon. Bī'a?"

Their mother leaned forward. "Yes?"

"Is there a guard with our horses?"

Celou felt a warm pride at her little brother's words. He had barely ten grasses, ten summers of life, yet he spoke like a man of great courage. The Crow had not hurt them yet, but as soon as there were horses stolen back, and wounded pride to consider, they could easily change their minds.

Celou heard her mother whispering to Jean-Paul, explaining about the roan. Celou gave the cradleboard the gentlest of pushes and heard Mu'mbič settle back to sleep as it swung back and forth.

"Where is the roan?" Bī'a asked in a barely audible whisper. She was on her feet now, swaying, working her muscles and grimacing at the cramps.

Celou pointed, telling her about the plum thicket.

"You carry Mu'mbič. And Jean-Paul will go with you. We will need another horse."

"Bī'a," Celou began, but her mother hissed quietly, cutting her off. *Go,* she signed. *Go now. Swift, down the hills to home. I will follow you.*

"One of them lost his bah-park," Celou whispered in a rush of words. Then she switched to sign. *I found it.*

Where?

"I hid it in a tree," Celou whispered.

Her mother waved one hand to show she had heard. Then she reached out to take the knife from Celou's belt. Holding it loosely, she waited while Jean-Paul struggled to his feet. He took a swaying step, then another, then came back.

Bī'a brushed her lips across Celou's cheek, then Jean-Paul's. She looked longingly at Mu'mbič, but Celou knew she would not risk waking him. Then she made a shooing gesture with one hand.

Celou reached up to the cradleboard. Swinging it lightly, she shrugged the strap over her shoulders. Then she put one arm around Jean-Paul. Bī'a smiled and lifted the knife. "I will follow if I can." Then she was gone in the darkness.

CHAPTER THIRTEEN

To Celou the meadow seemed endlessly wide. Jean-Paul was stiff and sore. His usually quick stride was slow and uneven. Mu'mbič's cradleboard bumped at the back of Celou's thighs. The shoulder strap was too long for her and she had to keep hitching it higher.

Celou was sweating again, from fear. The grasses seemed to shout, crackling beneath their feet and slapping loudly at their legs. The cradleboard creaked a little as she moved, a sound she had never noticed before. Jean-Paul coughed quietly, covering his mouth with both hands to mute the sound. Yet the lodges remained quiet; no one stirred.

Celou felt her hair tickle at her cheek and realized a little wind had come up, rattling the grass stems and moving the tree branches. Not all of the noise was theirs. She said a little prayer of gratitude and tried to quicken their pace. Jean-Paul was slow and clumsy. He kept pressing one hand to the swollen side of his face, but he made no sound, no complaint.

Once they were across the clearing, Celou stood looking up the slope. It seemed even steeper than when she had come down it. Jean-Paul hobbled forward, taking gimpy little steps, his hands balled into fists of pain. The rawhide had tightened as it had dried. It would take days for the soreness to go out of his ankles and wrists. Celou followed him closely.

The weight of the cradleboard made Celou lean forward, trying to keep her balance on the slope. She walked half bent, her eyes on the ground, trying not to stumble. So when Jean-Paul faltered, she bumped into him, thrusting her arms out to steady him. Instead, she knocked him sideways. She watched her brother fall, sprawling— almost rolling down the hill. He hit without a sound and she saw him splay his fingers to stop himself from sliding. Without a word, he managed to get up again, the swirling breeze covering the worst of the noise as sand and pebbles slid around his feet and hands.

Celou urgently gestured him onward. Jean-Paul could not hear it over the sighing of the wind through the grass, but Mu'mbič was murmuring again, stirring in his sleep. Celou pointed over her shoulder at the cradleboard and Jean-Paul turned uphill, placing his feet carefully, but managing to go a little faster.

At the top of the rise, Celou hesitated. Turning, she scanned the clearing for her mother. The moon had climbed in the sky and was so bright that Celou saw faint shadows stretching away from the lodges. From where she stood now, she could see over the thickets at the far side of the clearing. She could see the horses, even, vague outlines in the moonlight, but not the guard. The little wind was dying. The clearing was still.

Mu'mbič made a soft cry that spun her around, furious with herself for standing stupidly. She stumbled into Jean-Paul and he fell. Below, in the clearing, she heard a voice, quiet and questioning. A man's voice.

"Follow me," Celou whispered.

Jean-Paul scrambled to his feet and they started off, Celou leading the way. Behind them, she heard another voice, louder, then a cry, then the sound of several more voices. Someone shouted.

"Hurry," she hissed at Jean-Paul, hooking one arm beneath his and trying to steady him.

"Where is the roan?" he asked. His voice was uneven.

"Below that thicket," Celou answered, pointing.

She shoved Jean-Paul along. Where was their mother? Hiding? Perhaps she could crawl into the thicket and let the Crow think she had escaped. Or, perhaps, Celou thought, she had been in the open when the warriors had come pouring out of the brush lodges.

"Where?" Jean-Paul asked again.

Celou stared into the murky, moonlit trees where she had left the roan. For a heartbeat she couldn't see him and fear raked at her spine. Then the gelding raised his head to look at them, and she exhaled in explosive relief.

"Hurry," she said again, even though Jean-Paul was already running, a clumsy, stumbling gait. The cradleboard was banging against her back. Mu'mbič was awake and crying. It was hard for Celou to hear anything else, but she knew the shouts had not stopped.

With shaking hands, Celou undid the tie rope and boosted her brother onto the roan's back. There were hoofbeats now. She glanced back to see a pinto horse burst over the rim of the hill. She faced the roan again. As she jumped up, feeling Jean-Paul's hands on her shoulders pulling her across the roan's withers, she let herself believe that they still had a chance. The pinto had been riderless. That meant at least part of the herd was scattered. Her mother had managed that much. Some of the warriors would be horseless, at least until morning.

Hauling the roan around, Celou looked back one more time. There were three or four horses at the top of the rise now, all of them riderless, slowing to a trot, their heads high and tossing wildly. The roan started downhill as more horses crested the rise. Four of them galloped off at an angle, kicking up their heels in the cool night air. The moonlight cast pale silver over a single rider on the fifth horse. Her mother.

"Here, Bī'a," Celou shouted, then wished she could snatch her voice back out of the air and stuff it back down into her foolish throat. More horses were topping the slope. Just behind her mother rode three warriors.

Foolish or not, Celou knew that her voice had carried. Her mother veered, leaning forward on her horse's neck like a brave in a race. A sharp roar rang out and Celou flinched. One of the warriors had a gun. Her mother's black mare shied, but came on, galloping, plunging down the slope.

"Give me Mu'mbič," Celou heard her shout.

As her mother reined in, Celou was shrugging off the straps of the cradleboard. She leaned out to pass her brother to her mother, then waited just long enough to see that Bī'a had managed to slide one arm into the strap.

"Hold onto me," Celou screamed at Jean-Paul, and she felt his arms tighten around her waist. The roan was already turning, already leaping into a gallop as she pulled on the rein and leaned forward. She wrapped one hand in his mane and let the rein go slack, trusting his eyes, his instincts more than her own. She turned back to look. The Crow warriors were only five or six strides behind them.

Celou clung to the roan's back, watching the ground before them, trying to add her balance to his as he skidded and plunged, his forelegs absorbing the shock of the uneven downhill gallop. His head was up, his rear quarters bunched up beneath him. Celou rode as she had been taught, her arms close to her body, her legs tight on the roan's sides.

A shriek from behind them told her that one of the Crow's mounts had gone down and she turned to look back, catching a glimpse of the horse rolling, the rider hitting hard. The shriek had been from the horse, she realized, seeing it lie still, one foreleg at an unnatural angle.

Terror clawing at her, Celou faced front again. The pounding of the roan's hooves slowed as the ground steepened even more. Celou could just see her mother's black mare, light-footed and agile. The black was a good mount. Celou felt Jean-Paul's balance shift and she had to lean to compensate. Somehow, the roan kept his rhythm and went on without losing ground.

They came into a meadow and as the ground leveled, the horses lengthened their strides. The roan flattened out, his head lowering as he picked up speed. Here, his long, ground-eating stride would begin to tell. He was her father's favorite for very good reasons.

Celou kept her weight forward, forcing Jean-Paul to lie flat against her back. As the moonlit ground streamed beneath them, the roan slowly narrowed the lead Bī'a's mare had begun with. Celou kept glancing back.

There were two warriors still behind them. Both were riding hard, pushing their horses mercilessly. One of them rode with a tomahawk raised above his head. Neither, as far as Celou could see, had a gun. The rider whose horse had fallen must have been the one who had shot.

Over the pounding of the hoofbeats, Celou could hear Mu'mbič crying. The jolting ride was more than he could stand. She wanted to scream at the Crow warriors to stop, to turn back, to leave them alone.

Celou saw her mother turn and raise one hand, gesturing ahead. She faced forward and strained to see in the moonlight. But before she could see what her mother had meant, she felt it. The land dropped sharply and the roan had to shorten his strides to plunge downward again.

Bī'a twisted around to look back and held the knife high in the air, like a young warrior riding back into camp after a good battle. Her hair was wild, a dark halo around her face. She was shouting something Celou did not understand until she felt the heavy hand on her shoulder. One of the Crow had ridden fast enough to come up beside her.

Startled, Celou tried to shrug from beneath his grip, but could not. Turning, she could see Red-fringe, his face contorted with fury and concentration. He held her with his right hand. In his left was a rawhide quirt that whistled with the force of his blows as he whipped his laboring horse. He was desperate to get closer, a little better grip, so that he could drag her from the roan's back.

Gathering a handful of the roan's mane, Celou wrenched to the side. The warrior's grip loosened, but he only tightened it again, his fingers crawling forward on her shoulder like spider legs, one, then the next, his grip strengthening, the long red-tipped fringe on his shirt spilling over her back.

Celou screamed at Jean-Paul to let go of her waist. His arms only tightened at the sound of her voice. She shouted at him again, and this time the sense of her words must have reached him because he loosened his hold on her waist. She felt his whole body jerk and realized that he had probably been riding with his eyes closed, pressed against her back. He had not seen the Crow coming, had not known the ermine fringe tickling at him was not his sister's flying hair.

Jean-Paul began beating at Red-fringe's arm, biting him, but it did no good. Like the grip of one of her father's steel beaver traps, the Crow warrior clung relentlessly to Celou's shoulder, forcing her to slow the roan or be dragged off at a full gallop.

Celou reined in, thinking furiously. She waited until the roan was barely cantering, her mother watching helplessly from a little ways ahead. Then she found Jean-Paul's hand and pressed the single rein into it, balling his fist around the leather. Gripping the strap well above his hand, she pulled hard and the roan reared back, sliding to a stop.

"Ride!" Celou yelled at Jean-Paul. Then, without warning, she swung her leg over the roan's neck and dropped to the ground, running, stumbling, crashing to her knees. She heard the warrior curse as his horse shied to one side to avoid trampling her.

Celou saw Jean-Paul slide forward on the roan's back, turning around to watch her fall. She yelled at him, but he was still reining in, still half sideways, watching. Then the second warrior came up from behind, and Jean-Paul gave the roan his head again and went on down the slope.

Celou managed to get to her feet and, waving her arms and shrieking at the top of her lungs, brought the second warrior's horse to a head-tossing stop. He cursed at her, raising the tomahawk high, shouting at his companion.

Red-fringe drove his horse forward, slamming his fist into Celou's back as she turned to shield her face. She fell, spinning, the breath forced from her body.

Choking and gagging, Celou got to her feet, a sharp pain in one knee. Red-fringe was riding toward her again, his face a mask of murderous rage. She stood still, facing him, her head high and her heart slamming at her ribs. As he came she made a sign, moving slowly so he would be sure to see it clearly.

I know where, she told him with her gesture. *I know where*. Then, very deliberately, she touched the base of her own throat, mimicking the gesture she had seen him make so many times. She saw the second warrior reining in, his face puzzled as he watched her. She signed again, touching her throat a second time, her eyes fastened on Red-fringe's. He reined in his horse, bringing it to a plunging halt a few paces from her. Then he swung down to the ground and walked toward her.

Celou wanted to turn, to see if Jean-Paul was safely astride the roan, racing to freedom behind their mother, but she was afraid to take her eyes off the Crow. He was staring at her, his glare as intense as fire heat. He stopped in front of her and waited, motionless except for the convulsive tightening and loosening of his right hand.

Celou repeated her signs one more time. The warrior jutted his hand out from his shoulder, tipping the thumb upward two or three times: the question sign. Then he pointed at random, his gesture impatient, jabbing. *Where?*

While Red-fringe glared at her, Celou gave in to her impulse and turned to look. There, at the limit of her vision in the moonlight, her mother and Jean-Paul were disappearing into the night. Her mother would not stop, she was sure. Once her sons were safe with her family, she would come back, with or without help. But not before.

Celou felt her legs begin to shake as though the jump from the roan's back had taken all her courage and left her empty of anything but fear.

The warrior's face was ugly in his rage, the moon-light highlighting the furrows in his brow, the sharp angle of his cheeks.

Where? Bah-park? He used the throat-touch gesture she had to frame the question. *Mine,* he signed, turning the gesture into an accusation, as though she had stolen the medicine bundle from him.

Celou looked up and down the mountainside, now unnaturally still and quiet as the pounding hooves faded below them. The truth was, she wasn't sure where she had hidden his bah-park. But even if her marked tree was below them, she was not about to lead him in the direction her family had gone. She pointed upslope, trying to look confident. He frowned, staring into her face. She looked aside, wondering if he could see, in the moonlight, that her eyes were blue. Abruptly, he gestured for her to start walking.

CHAPTER FOURTEEN

Celou led the way in the moonlight. Both warriors dismounted and walked behind her, talking in low voices. She could understand a few words, but they made no sense strung together. She heard the word "tibo" several times, which let her know that the moonlight was bright enough to reveal her blue eyes to Red-fringe. Or perhaps her mother's dress had been enough. Maybe they were worried about making her father angry. She hoped so.

As she walked, she listened for hoofbeats from above, but none came. Her mother must have managed to scatter the Crows' small band of horses well. The other warriors were still afoot, stuck in camp with the women. The moon was high overhead now, the horses would be able to travel far and fast if they wanted to—Celou prayed that they would. With luck, it would take the Crow most of the next day or two to recover even part of their horses. If

Shoshone riders found them first—or the Blackfoot, on their way home, the Crow would never get them all back.

A harsh word from Red-fringe made Celou look around. He was glaring at her, making a shooing motion with one hand. Celou turned back and walked a little faster, trying hard to look like she knew where she was going. She angled across the slope and walked along the far side of the open ground for awhile, then crossed back.

Another grating sound made her turn around to face the warriors again. Red-fringe had mounted his horse. His friend was swinging up as she turned.

There was a quick exchange of words between the two men. Then, Red-fringe faced her as the other warrior rode away without looking back. Celou watched him leave, her hands balled into anxious fists until he turned upslope, not down. Were they giving up on recapturing her family? It was possible, Celou thought.

The Crow warriors had not bargained for so much trouble from a woman and her children. If they were part of a hunting group, they might just recapture their horses, count themselves lucky to have ended up with three extra, then hurry to catch up with their main party. Celou felt a pang of regret that her little dark bay mare was lost.

She turned and glanced at Red-fringe. He was staring at her. *Where?* he signed. Then he touched his throat.

Celou looked upslope. She had apparently headed in the right direction, at least. Even in the moonlight, the rocks were whiter above them. She started across the clearing again, then whirled around when Red-fringe spoke sharply to her in Crow. She waited for him to sign, but he only made his fly-shooing motion, telling her to go on.

It was not long before Celou saw the split boulder, her place keeper. But she did not turn toward the aspen tree that held the bah-park; she knew that every delay gave her family time to flee toward home. Once he had his medicine back, there was nothing to make Red-fringe stay here.

Celou slowed her step and looked upslope, as though she were confused. Then she started off again, walking so slowly that Red-fringe had to stop his horse and let her get a little ahead before riding on. She heard him mutter behind her.

Wait here, Celou signed, turning. *It is not far.*

Then, without giving him a chance to react, she turned from the open ground into the trees. She looked back, walking slowly, gesturing vaguely ahead of herself as though she was too exhausted to do more than stumble along. It wasn't hard to pretend.

Her legs were heavy with fatigue. And she was hungry and thirsty.

And none of this matters, she thought as she came closer to the thick stand of pines she had spotted. The best thing she could do for herself and her family now was to make Red-fringe spend the rest of the night thinking about his lost bah-park. The moon would slide down the far side of the sky. The sun would come up. When it did, she wanted Red-fringe to still be wandering in the woods, too busy to think about the swift mare her mother had stolen back, galloping side by side with her father's roan, all the way home.

Red-fringe shouted at her. She could see him signing out of the corner of her eye. He was demanding to know how much farther they had to go. Celou glanced toward the stand of pines.

These were young lodgepole pines, the kind most people used for their tipis, straight and tall, with their slim trunks close together. But there was something odd. The pines were all about the same age, and growing thickly as they usually did after a fire had cleared the way for them to sprout. But there was no sign of fire as she got closer. The ground between the lodgepoles wasn't darkened with years-old ash. It was a maze of fallen logs like stick-dice dropped from someone's hand, stuck at crazy angles, half buried in the matted layers of brown pine needles.

Celou noticed a pattern in the deadfalls, as if a giant hand had knocked down all the trees in one direction. Her grandfather had shown Jean-Paul a place like this once, and Jean-Paul had described it to her. There were winds sometimes, contained in the long arm of a cloud. These winds were strong enough to lay the trees down like knife-cut grass.

The more Celou looked, the surer she was that this was such a place. The seedlings had grown up through the debris years before and were becoming tall trees in their own right. But there was almost no open ground beneath them—it was all piles of rotting trunks and brittle limbs.

Celou took three or four more slow, labored steps, making her decision. If she had a chance to escape Red-fringe, it would be in a place like this one. Without warning, she leaped into the trees. Red-fringe's curses ringing in her ears, she ducked under one of the old fallen trees that had landed at an angle, lying crosswise on top of four or five others. Just beyond it, an enormous rock jutted upward with young pines growing on all sides. Celou scrambled over it, sliding down the far side on her bottom.

The Crow warrior shouted once more, then

went silent. Celou moved as fast as she could, without a single look backward, knowing that any hesitation would be a mistake. Whatever head start she had gotten would soon be eliminated by the warrior's longer legs, once he was off his horse and following her. But he was bigger, and once he was deep into the stand of windfall trees, the small spaces would be harder for him to get through.

Without slowing, Celou half turned. She could not see Red-fringe in the moonlight, but she could hear him, could hear the twigs breaking, the brittle deadwood shattering beneath his feet as he crashed through the woods behind her.

She bent double, finding a way through the jumble of fallen logs, then turned to crawl into the inky darkness under a thick, rotting lodgepole trunk, wedged at a slant close to the ground. Making her way forward on all fours, Celou picked the smallest places she could see, one after another. Breathing hard, she belly-crawled, shinned, and squeezed herself farther and farther into the wind-slaughtered trees.

When she finally slowed, her heart slamming at her ribs, she couldn't hear Red-fringe behind her anymore. Afraid to believe that he had given up pursuit so easily, Celou pushed her way between two logs, the rotten wood crunching beneath her weight. Then she stopped altogether again, listening. On all sides of her, deadwood and pine needles lay in almost impenetrable piles, layered in silence.

Celou began to smile, suppressing giddy laughter. She had gotten away from Red-fringe. She had found, by sheer good fortune, the one place in the woods where her small size had given her an advantage he could not match.

Celou tipped her head back and grinned. Her father would be very proud of her if she lived to tell him all she had done this night. So would Bī'a. Jean-Paul would be embarrassed in front of his friends, having such a sister, one who did boys' deeds. But he would be proud of her in secret, she thought. Mu'mbič would hear the story a hundred times, growing up. He would probably hate being reminded that he was the baby, the one they all had to carry, to care for . . . Celou brought her thoughts up short. Gloating over a victory not yet won was foolish.

The forest was silent, but it probably meant nothing except that Red-fringe was listening now, too. Celou looked around the place she had decided to stop. It reminded her of the traders' cabins around Fort Henry. Her father had trapped that country when she was little, and she remembered the tibo's lodges, squatty, square, and dark, the logs piled one atop the next one, in sad brown rows.

Celou leaned forward and rested her forehead on her knees, trying to think. She was not safe yet. She knew that. But she had a chance now. And so did her family if Red-fringe would only keep searching for her, for his bah-park, not mount up and ride after them.

Just as she thought his name, Celou heard a popping sound in the woods upslope from where she sat. She straightened. Upslope? She heard more of the rotten wood shatter, then a heavy thud.

Celou huddled back against the log she had crawled beneath, pressing herself into the shadows. All her giddy joy dissolved. Red-fringe was not hurrying, he was not cursing—nor was he trying to be quiet. His progress through the log maze was steady and measured. His calmness frightened Celou. She rolled onto her hands and knees and closed her eyes to concentrate on listening.

He was coming closer. His steps seemed purposeful, without hesitation. He seemed to know which direction she had taken. Had he waited at the edge of the trees, tracking her with his ears until she stopped? Of course. He hadn't been foolish enough to chase her, drowning out her noise with his own.

Celou knew that the instant she moved, he

would be able to stop again and listen, keeping track of her direction. There was no way to pass silently through these woods. But if she stayed where she was, there would be no escape when he found her. She remembered the heavy grip of his hand on her shoulder and shivered.

Celou listened, knowing how a rabbit must feel, hearing the wolf approach, but knowing that to dart out of cover meant an even more certain death. Staying still gave her a small chance. Red-fringe might go around her by mistake. He might miss seeing her, or pass within arm's reach. But only if she could be as silent as the night itself.

Flattening herself against the logs, Celou braced her body carefully, moving each arm, then each leg so slowly that the first tiny crackle of twig or rotten bark was the last. Everything depended on silence now.

Celou heard the creaking of rotten wood. Was he lifting a log? Every rustle seemed like the roar of gunfire. The footsteps paused, then came on again. Celou closed her eyes. He was close. More steps and another pause. He was so close she could hear him swallow.

Celou lowered her head, unable to do anything else. Another step, so close that the crackling seemed to come from the other side of the logs she leaned against. Celou held her breath. Suddenly, the logs behind her shifted and she felt his clutching hand on her back. She reacted violently, rolling away, struggling to get up. But he had a handful of her hair, and this time his grip was iron strong, relentless. He hauled her to her feet.

Celou stared up at him. In the waning moonlight his face was dark, unreadable. But his signs were perfectly clear. He wanted his bah-park. She would not try to escape again. If she valued her life, she would get the bah-park for him now. NOW.

Celou let him push her along, working her way back out of the pine maze. But once they were on open ground, and he had remounted his horse, she stood still, refusing to lead him anywhere. After he had his bah-park, there would be no bargaining with him. This would be her last chance.

I go home, she signed. *Your bah-park. Trade.* She looked at the ground, then risked a glance at his face. The moon was sinking low on the horizon, the shadows were too deep to see his intent in his eyes.

Red-fringe did not immediately agree, which encouraged Celou. If he were going to betray her, he would not take so much time to decide—he would just lie and be quick about it. When he finally signed agreement, Celou felt a weight come off her heart as hope lifted some of her fear.

Maybe he was an honorable man. Many Crow were good for their word, her father said. When there was not trouble between the Crow and the Shoshone, he liked trading with the Crow. He said their fur packs were almost always full count, full weight, and honest.

Celou walked slowly this time because the weariness of the long night's fear and tension was settling onto her shoulders. She led Red-fringe away from the edge of the forest and walked back down the slope. The moon was setting now. In a little while it would be very dark.

The white rocks were harder to see with the moon falling, but the big split boulder was visible. Celou walked to it and stood beside it. Red-fringe reined in, glaring at her. He signed at her.

Where?

His face was set, fierce with impatience.

Here?

Even his signing was jagged, jabbing gestures that let her know his questions were angry demands. His hair had come free of the bound bundle at the nape of his neck. It spilled down his back, longer than Bī'a's had been before she cut it. Celou remembered her father talking about a Crow named Yellow Hand who had hair longer than his height. If it was not bundled up each day, it would have dragged the ground.

Red-fringe made an impatient sound in his throat, and Celou turned and slowly made her way to the aspen trees that grew to one side of the split boulder. She saw her mark and the stone and pine cone atop it.

The bear tree was taller than Celou remembered. It seemed to take a long time for her to work her way up into the branches. Then it took more time for her to spot the bah-park. The thongs were still tightly tied and she had to change her position twice, steadying herself so she could free both hands to work at them.

When she had the little rawhide bundle free of the limb, she looked down at Red-fringe. She could not see his face clearly. The moon sat just on the horizon to the west now, its light dim and waning fast. Celou took a deep breath, weary, wishing she could just stay up in the tree forever.

The Crow said something to her. His words were a meaningless torrent of sound to her, but his message was easily understood. He was tired of waiting, anxious to hold his warrior's medicine in his hands again. Celou shifted her grip on the smooth white bark of the aspen. The stars glittered overhead and the air was cold now.

If she refused to come down, he would force her somehow, cutting the tree down with his hatchet if he had to, or drawing an arrow to shoot her out of it like a hunted bird. A shiver ran through the tree and startled Celou out of her thoughts. Redfringe had shaken the trunk and was glaring up at her now. Another torrent of Crow words shoved at her ears. She started downward.

CHAPTER FIFTEEN

Celou hesitated just out of Red-fringe's reach. His horse was tethered close. An idea formed in her mind. She pretended to slip and caught herself, knowing she had to make it look real. Red-fringe was not a fool. She pretended again to lose her balance, crying out as though it had frightened her. She gripped the tree trunk like a child of five grasses and looked down at him.

Red-fringe said something in Crow. He pointed at the ground.

"I am trying to come down," Celou said in Shoshone. Her voice sounded scared and weak, not because she was pretending, but because she was terrified. This was the kind of trick her father would call fool's play. It could so easily go wrong. But what else could she do? She was afraid to trust him.

"I am trying," she repeated, struggling awkwardly to shift her footholds. This time, she let the bah-park dangle down where he could see it.

Red-fringe stepped forward, reaching up. He said something in Crow, a single short word. It was not difficult for Celou to guess what it meant. "I'm falling," she screamed suddenly, letting herself slip. She whipped her free arm around as though she was trying to catch herself. The thong attached to the bah-park stung her wrist. She flailed again. This time, as her arm went out, Celou let go of the bah-park. She cried out and pointed, looking in the direction it had gone. There was a tiny rustle in the trees a little ways off. The bah-park had found a new hiding place.

Furious, Red-Fringe shook the tree, hard. Celou grabbed the trunk, her cheek grating on the bark, barely hanging on. Then she listened to him curse as he turned to follow the sound in the dark. Celou watched him get one step away from the tree, then two. He passed his tethered horse and kept going.

Celou leapt to the ground, fear making her as quick and graceful as a mountain cat. In three long steps she was at the horse's side. An instant later she was on it, whipping it into a gallop, thundering down the hill.

In the last of the moonlight, she heard him shout, glanced back to see him lift his bow. But if he shot, she never knew it. When the night had swallowed her and his shouts had died, she reined in and went on at a safer pace.

Halfway down the mountain, she stopped to let the horse drink in a creek that sounded like jingling brass bells as it tumbled over the stones in its path. The dark seemed like a friend to her now, the night warm and soft. Remounting, Celou felt happy, peaceful. She was not afraid of ghosts this night, she realized, or anything else. When the sun came up, she welcomed its warmth as much as its light.

Celou's family was not at the tipi, but she had not expected them to be. As she rode into the big camp, she saw men lying here and there, wounds covered with moss to keep the flies out. Already the women had piled the burned tipi poles near the fire pits and had made brush shelters for their families with whatever the Blackfoot had left them to work with.

"Your mother is at her uncle's lodge!" Celou turned to see Tsi'dzi standing with her hands on her hips. "Is it true you went into the Crow camp alone?" Her voice was full of admiration.

Celou nodded, unsure what to say. Just then, she heard Bī'a cry out with joy and turned to see her mother running toward her. Sliding off Red-fringe's horse, Celou embraced Bī'a. "Jean-Paul?" she asked.

"He is sleeping," Bī'a told her. "And Mu'mbič. We will stay here until your father comes home."

Celou allowed herself to smile, to begin to truly believe her family was safe. Her mother leaned close. "Jean-Paul has told his friends about how brave you were. They have told everyone."

"There is more to tell," Celou whispered to her mother.

Bī'a took her arm. "Jean-Paul will also want to hear."

Together they walked across the camp, Celou leading Red-fringe's horse past people who stopped to stare at her as they always had. But this morning, they were smiling.

August 8, 1826, at our tipi, ready to move down to the big camp.

Jean-Paul is jealous of what he calls my victory over the Crow warriors. Papa will say God was with me, I know. Bī'a says the coyotes helped us, made us clever.

Red-fringe and his friends might have seen the Blackfoot, Bī'a says, then just happened upon our lodge and decided to trade away their bad beaver pelts. Maybe then they realized how easy it would be to take our horses if the Blackfoot attacked the big camp, so they came back. Jean-Paul says we will never know the truth, to stop talking about it. He is better today, only his skull aches terribly.

Papa will be angry about the grays and my bay mare. Jean-Paul cannot remember what happened to his buckskin. Maybe we will find it wandering the mountainside, dragging its rein. Papa will be very glad none of us are badly hurt. Bī'a says they will have to argue again because Papa will want us to go live at a trading post now. She says she will never live in a wood house, that they are dark and smell bad. I have never wanted to live in the big camp, but I would like it better than a trading post, I think. Some of the girls act like they want to be my friends now. No one has teased me about my eyes since I returned.

My feet hurt today, all the cuts are pink and they sting. I wish there was no work to do, but we must load the travois and move everything down to the big camp.

Mu'mbič is laughing at something he sees. Perhaps a bird. His cradleboard is hanging from a cottonwood branch. He would not like living in a wood house either. Nor Jean-Paul. Jean-Paul says he likes living in the winter caves the best. Papa has told us there are wood houses and stone houses and houses made of baked clay. I want to see every kind of house before I decide which I want when I am grown. Bī'a is waiting for help. I will write more later. Perhaps Papa will come home tomorrow. I hope so.

Sometimes one day can change a life forever

AMERICAN *Diaries*

Different girls,
living in different periods of America's past
reveal their hearts' secrets in the pages
of their diaries. Each one faces a challenge
that will change her life forever.
Don't miss any of their stories:

#1 ❧ *Sarah Anne Hartford*
#2 ❧ *Emma Eileen Grove*
#3 ❧ *Anisett Lundberg*
#4 ❧ *Mary Alice Peale*
#5 ❧ *Willow Chase*
#6 ❧ *Ellen Elizabeth Hawkins*
#7 ❧ *Alexia Ellery Finsdale*
#8 ❧ *Evie Peach*
#9 ❧ *Celou Sudden Shout*
#10 ❧ *Summer McCleary*

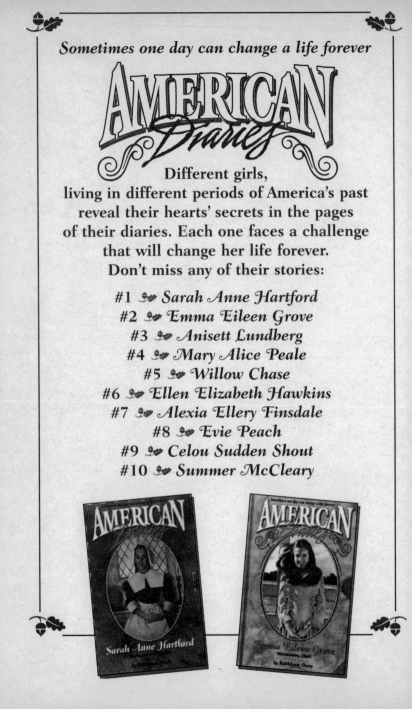